WISH YOU KNEW

JULIE ARCHER

To Toby Tarrant...
for playing banging tunes
during lockdown
which helped me write
all the words

PLAYLIST

I Wish You Knew - Caggie
Fell in Love with a Girl - The White Stripes
Nothing Breaks Like A Heart - Frank Carter & The
Rattlesnakes
Falling Asleep At The Wheel - Holly Humberstone
Animals - Maroon 5
Ever Fallen in Love (With Someone You Shouldn't've) -
Buzzcocks
RadioX - mostly between 10am and 1pm on weekdays

1

SCOTT

Don't think I can't see your green eyes from here, Rosie Tatton.

It wasn't the first occasion my gaze had strayed to my ex, chatting to her best friend over the other side of the bar.

Meeting fans after a gig still counted as one of my favourite things. I enjoyed meeting them, particularly those who had supported us since the start. And I *loved* meeting our female followers too. Okay, yeah, it was mostly about the women. The dozen people crowded around me were all women, and I could see Rosie shooting daggers in my direction. Her reaction always intrigued me. We'd dated for a few weeks last year, until I'd fucked it up by shagging someone from *Love Island* at a party at her house. Understandably, she'd been pissed off, but it hadn't stopped her and I from hooking up whenever we were in the same place at the same time ever since.

Like tonight.

I held her in my eye line for a moment longer, wondering whether the opportunity would present itself.

The intimate event for the release of my band's latest single at The Matchbox in Manchester had gone without a hitch. Unlike the last time we'd been here, which had set off a chain of events surrounding Saff Barnes and her boyfriend, but that was another story. There were around a hundred or so Trash Gun and TheSB fans, plus the usual entourage which came with two bands putting on a gig, as well as friends and family.

Someone put another beer in my hand. I gratefully accepted it as a voice in my ear grated louder.

"Can we go yet, Scott? I'm bored and there's a really good vibe down at Cinnamon."

I swigged from the bottle, reluctantly turning my attention away from Rosie to the woman I didn't remember agreeing to go anywhere with. "What's Cinnamon?"

The brunette rolled her eyes. "And you say you know all the clubs around here."

"All the rock clubs, for sure, babe." I grinned. "I'm guessing Cinnamon doesn't fall into that category."

She huffed and finished off the last of her wine. "Can we get more drinks instead then?" She shoved the glass into my chest.

Grudgingly, I waved to the bar staff to get her a fresh drink. I think I'd spoken about five words to her since we'd arrived. Now, she was clingier than the bandage dress wrapped around her over-generous curves.

The angel in me told me I ought to take her to one side, let her down gently, and then she could piss off to

Cinnamon and find some other unsuspecting bloke to pin her attentions on.

The devil in me caught sight of Rosie again, and suddenly the woman was pressed flush to my side, and we were on our way over to her and Saff.

What the fuck was I doing?

"All right, ladies? Having a good night?" I asked.

Rosie feigned disinterest. "We were until you came over." She lifted her champagne glass to her lips and took a delicate sip.

My dick twitched at the memory of those lips and the talents they possessed. The devil in me nudged me right in the balls.

Saff elbowed the woman out of the way and threw her arms around me. "Honestly, Scott, thank you. There have been times in the last few weeks when I really should have punched you, but it all seems to have worked out for the best."

My mouth stretched into a smile and we drew apart. "You probably should have." I paused. "I am sorry about everything."

Saff clutched her chest. "What? Scott Lincoln apologising for something?" She turned to Rosie. "Note the date and time, that's going down in history."

Rosie's face remained impassive, but I could tell she was desperate to know the story between me and whatever-her-name-was.

"Yeah, yeah, funny." I mocked. "Tris is a decent guy. You're good together."

"As if I'd ever be interested in you, right, Rosie?" Saff grinned.

Her cheeks pinked as Saff nudged her in the ribs. I raised my eyebrows.

"I can't imagine what she'd see in you compared to Tris." Rosie finally met my gaze, her gorgeous eyes - actually blue, not green - sparkling with mischief, rather than the jealousy I'd seen in them earlier. "Right now, I can't think of a single thing you have going for you." She ran a tongue over her lips.

Fuck.

Why was I even entertaining the idea of taking someone I barely knew to a club I knew I'd hate, when my ex-slash-friend-with-benefits appeared to be making a play for me?

Stalling for time, I turned to the woman. "Didn't you say something about meeting your friends?"

Her brows knotted together. "No..."

"Sure you did, isn't it time you went?" I made a play of air kissing her on both cheeks. "It's been fun, but we both know it isn't going anywhere."

The sting of fizzy liquid in my eyes made it obvious she hadn't taken my dismissal well. Rosie's hand flew to her mouth, trying to cover up a bout of giggles. Saff's jaw dropped. I shook my head, and wiped my eyes, blinking. "Wow. Classy."

"You're an absolute prick!" The woman yelled in my face.

"Can't argue with that," muttered Rosie, under her breath.

"At least I'm being honest, babe. Imagine if I'd slept with you first, then dropped you. How cheap would you have felt?" I was doing everything to live up to the popular perception of me.

"Oh my God, did you really say that?" She threw the empty glass to the floor, causing it to shatter at our feet. "I'm leaving before I do or say something I'll really regret. I thought you'd be different." Without another word, she flounced away.

I breathed a sigh of relief.

Saff sucked in her lips. "Ouch."

"Come on, it was the truth and you know it. I did the right thing in getting her to leave now, before she humiliated herself."

"Because you did that for her," snapped Rosie. "You really are a prick." She turned on her heels and stalked off, giving me an exquisite view of her arse encased in tight black leather jeans.

I did it because of you, Rosie, I wanted to say. But she was already walking away.

"What the hell was that all about?" Saff frowned.

I let my head fall back and stared up at the ceiling, still stained with cigarette smoke even after all these years. "Fucked if I know."

It had already been an interesting evening. I'd have been happy for it to end with me and Rosie going off somewhere, but it didn't look like that was on the cards. And when Tris whisked Saff away to their hotel, I was left alone like Billy No Mates.

I could have gone home, probably should have.

There was more than enough bait to take me away from reality, both in human and chemical form. I knew after the tour I should rein it in, take a break, let my body and mind recover.

I needed a lull, some respite from the excesses.

I needed a piss.

Stepping away from the bar, I thought about my planned trip to my mum and aunt's place. A whole week in the country, away from any stress and more importantly, away from any temptation.

A vision of Rosie Tatton walking away from me in those tight leather jeans filled my mind, and I grinned.

Talk about temptation.

As if I'd conjured her up, she appeared in front of me.

We stood in the centre of the hallway to the restrooms, people pushing past on either side.

"Hey," I said. She went to walk past me, but I caught her arm. "About earlier..."

"You don't have to explain. It's not as if I don't know your reputation." Rosie tossed back her mane of blonde hair. "Trying to make me jealous?"

"Damn, you got me." I hung my head in mock shame. Through the thin material of her top, I could see the outline of her erect nipples. The corner of my mouth curled up. "It's one of the things you love about me, right?"

Her amber eyes studied mine. "Love? As if."

"You staying in a hotel tonight?"

She nodded.

I grabbed her hand and pulled her towards me. "Then what are we waiting for?"

Beep. *Beep. Beep. Beeeeep.*

I cracked open an eyelid and reached for the phone to stop the alarm. What idiot agreed to a shoot the day after her best friend's release party? Had the shoot not been for a friend who owned an up and coming brand, I would have cried off. But the happy coincidence of being in Manchester, was something I couldn't turn down.

The bed next to me was empty, unsurprisingly. Scott would have gone by now, it was his thing, he never stayed the night. My thighs ached deliciously from our unexpected workout. I stretched back on the pillows.

Why did we always end up in bed?

Like he was a drug I couldn't quit, a habit that was impossible to break.

Despite everything, I was addicted to Scott Lincoln.

My phone pinged with a message to say the car would be coming to pick me up in around thirty minutes, enough time for a functional shower; the hair and make-up team would sort me out properly when I got there.

The shoot location was at a hotel in the centre of the city. The *SFU* team had commandeered the entire penthouse suite for the day.

"Rosie! I haven't seen you in ages!" Ellie Porley enveloped me in a huge hug. "I feel like you've been neglecting me, living your fancy London life instead of slumming it with me in Manchester."

I laughed as she released me. "I know, it's such a hard life, what with jet-setting across the globe for fancy modelling jobs." I put a hand to my brow in a show of mock dramatics.

"I'm honoured you agreed to bestow some love on little 'ol *SFU*," she said, carrying on the light-hearted banter.

SFU - aka *Sexy For U* - fought for much coveted space in the underwear market. Their mix of fun sportiness and classic sexiness was gaining in popularity. With me in this ad campaign, Ellie was convinced the brand would really take off. If I possessed the same level of arrogance as Scott, I would agree with her. The more modest side of me knew it would take more than a pretty blonde in a pair of lacy panties to really make it shine.

We chatted for a few more minutes until the male model taking part in the shoot arrived.

"Hey, Mark!" Ellie's enthusiasm didn't waver. "This is Rosie. Have you worked together before?"

"No," we answered at the same time.

I gave Mark a surreptitious once over. He looked like a typical Abercrombie model, blond hair, teeth and clean-cut muscles. Not my type. But then I was only doing an ad campaign with him, not giving myself over to him for the rest of my life.

"I'm looking forward to working with Rosie," he said. "She has a great portfolio."

His comment struck me as a little creepy, but I dismissed it. It wasn't totally out of left field for one model to compliment another.

"Hair and make-up are ready for you," Ellie said to me. "Shouldn't take long, then we can get started."

I headed over to the corner of the living area which had been set up as the dressing room, saying hello to the team who would be working their magic on me. While they began styling, I checked out the rail with the new range of garments. Bodysuits, bras and panties in a few different hues, hung next to boxers, briefs and trunks in similar shades.

Ellie decided to shoot the sporty sets first, the look fresh, almost innocent. Showcasing the cotton sets in pastel colours, my hair was pulled up in a bouncy ponytail, with natural lips and barely-there eyes. Mark and I laughed and joked with each other, occasionally embracing or touching as directed by the photographer. Sometimes working with a male model was awkward or uncomfortable, but he made it easy, making me relax.

Over lunch, we hung out, chatting and talking about other jobs we'd done.

"Who's the worst photographer you've ever worked with?" Mark asked.

"I couldn't possibly say! You never know when you

might work with them again. Plus, they might be your best friend and I'd offend you as well." I spooned some more yoghurt into my mouth. Photoshoot lunches had a tendency to be heavy on the carbs and after stuffing my hungover self with a couple of delicious bagels, dessert had to be something healthy. "Worst brand?"

Mark laughed. "Same answer you gave me. I'd never diss a brand because they know people who know people. Suddenly, your phone barely rings and you're scraping a living doing catalogue work." He looked down at his feet. "Kind of like I'm doing right now."

"Oh, really? I'm sorry. Working with *SFU* should give you a lift, right?" The majority of models I'd worked with in the past would never have been so open as to say they were struggling.

"Rosie?" Ellie came over to us. "Are you ready to shoot the other lingerie now?" She turned to Mark. "We don't need you for these shots, but you're welcome to hang around in case we need to reshoot anything from this morning."

"Right. Sure." The light mood disappeared, his shoulders slumped, and he sank back into the armchair.

I got up and followed Ellie over to the dressing area.

She pointed to the lingerie on the rail. "Your choice which to do when. There are three new ranges, a bodysuit, a bralette and a set, all in two colours. We'll see you on set when you're ready."

My fingers ran over the silky material of the items, each in simple black and white. Instinctively, I bet Scott would prefer the black version. I slid into the first bodysuit, lacy and embroidered at the top, delicate and sheer below the waistline. A perfect combination of elegance and brashness.

"Can we redo your hair and make-up?" called the hair-dresser from behind the screen which had been set up to separate off the dressing area.

"Sure, I'm pretty much ready."

The woman peeped around the side of the screen. "Wow, that looks incredible on you!"

I caught sight of my reflection in the mirror. The structured boning emphasised my breasts, and the high cut of the bottom elongated my legs. As I took a second look, I saw it through Scott's eyes and heat pooled in my groin, my insides contracting.

I had to stop thinking about him.

Shaking myself back to the present, I beckoned her in to work her magic again.

The afternoon session took longer than the morning one. I'd done the majority of shots on my own, but the photographer got Mark in for a few. Despite the work we'd done that morning, it had taken me a little while to get used to a virtual stranger holding me close and running his hands over my skin.

Finally, we were done. I pulled the robe around my body and headed over to see the initial results.

The photographer showed me some of the early rushes of the shots on his laptop.

"We'll do a few edits, not that there's much to do. These shots are amazing."

He wasn't wrong. I tugged the robe tighter around my body, heat flooding through me as I bent down to scan the screen. If only he knew I'd been fantasising about Scott Lincoln half the time to get the sexy, heavily hooded looks.

"Can you send me these?" I pointed at three of the best. "For Insta teasers? Promise not to show everything."

The photographer roared with laughter. "You're pretty much showing everything in them anyway."

I punched him on the arm. "I meant the products. Ellie will kill me if I reveal them before they go live."

He grinned. "I know. Gimme a sec and I'll email them over."

While he did so, I went back to the dressing room to find my clothes. Mark was already there, dressed in jeans, but yet to put on a shirt. His back was to me and I took the opportunity to check out his muscled back and shoulders. Hearing me enter, he turned around, giving me the chance to ogle his chest and abs again. Impressive, but disappointedly devoid of ink, unlike someone else I knew.

"Hey, Rosie. Good working with you, I had fun." He flashed his pearly whites.

"Yeah, me too. Perhaps we'll get to do it again."

He hesitated, then pulled a t-shirt on over his head. "Are you headed home after this?"

"No, staying over another night. I'm back to London in the morning. You?" I went over to the dressing table, grabbed a cleansing wipe and started to tone the make-up down.

"Same. Do you fancy grabbing a drink and something to eat?"

I considered my options. Saff and Tris had already gone back to London. My options were to go back to a dreary hotel room, order room service and watch crap reality television, or go out with Mark. The latter sounded much more appealing.

I nodded. "Sounds good. Give me a chance to get dressed and then we can head straight out?"

There was a short pause. "I need to pop back to my hotel and grab my wallet. Shall I meet you back here in about half an hour?"

"Sure, I'll wait for you outside."

Mark flashed me another megawatt smile. "Excellent, I'll see you soon."

As Mark exited, Ellie walked back in. "Bye, Mark, good working with you. We'll be in touch if there's any more work."

He smiled and thanked her.

She raised her eyebrows. "You two going out?"

"You can join us if you want."

"Love to, but I just popped in to say goodbye, I can't stay around. I've got a late meeting with a supplier." She embraced me. "We really need to sort out a proper catch up." Her eyes narrowed mischievously. "And you can give me all the gossip on your love life."

"What gossip? There isn't any." I rolled my eyes.

"There might be after tonight." She dodged out of my way, waving as she left the room. "Talk soon!"

Once Ellie had gone, I stripped out of the lingerie I'd been modelling. Somewhat disappointed I wasn't able to keep it, I wished I'd asked Ellie if I could. Once dressed in my own clothes, I had a few minutes to kill before going outside. I checked my emails to see if the photographer had sent through the pictures. He had. The shots, even without the edits, were amazing. I saved them to my phone and fired up my messaging app.

Rosie: Thought you'd like to see the results from today! Not bad considering the hangover from hell! See you back in London xxx

I pressed send. Saff would appreciate the message, she'd promised to help out with promo where she could.

Seconds later, I had a reply.

Scott: Fuck me, Rosie! Getting hard looking at these... You still in Manchester?

Shit. Shit. Shit.

Saff and Scott's details were next to each other in my contacts list.

I covered my eyes with my hand and winced.

Was it accidental? He had been on my mind throughout the day.

Rosie: Sorry! Not meant for your eyes. Can you delete?

Scott: Shame. Sure I can't keep them for my spank bank??

Rosie: NOOOOO!

Scott: And you never answered my question about where you were.

Rosie: Yes, I'm still in Manchester.

Scott: Want to...

I didn't even wait for him to complete the message before replying.

Rosie: Already going out with one of the guys from the shoot.

He didn't reply straight away and after several minutes of staring at my screen, waiting for the jumping dots to indicate a response, I gave up.

The make-up artist stuck her head into the room. "Rosie, are you ready to go? We're all packed up."

I gave the room a cursory sweep, checking I had all my stuff, and stood up. "Yes, all good. Are you guys going out too?"

"No, we've got another shoot in the morning, so getting an early night. You have fun with Mark." She winked.

I nodded in agreement. If I needed a distraction from Scott, he had to be it.

Two hours later, I wished I'd taken the option to stay in and order room service. Having been such a laugh during the course of the shoot, Mark turned out to be much less interesting in real life. We went to a vegan restaurant for dinner - he couldn't eat gluten either - and while I didn't disagree with people's choices, a plant-based burger didn't exactly meet my hungover, post-shoot cravings. When he suggested going to a bar for a nightcap, I didn't say no. At least I could get some crisps or pork scratchings.

The Bell was a bar around the corner from my hotel, which meant I wouldn't have too far to go when I finally called an end to the evening. Politeness said I'd need to spend at least another hour in his company before making a run for it.

Mark got the drinks, beer for him, a vodka and tonic for

me. I sipped the drink slowly, still feeling somewhat delicate. There was a strange taste to it, but I put that down to the fact he'd probably ordered some fancy tonic with an odd flavouring. I fished out the piece of cucumber contaminating it too.

"What's been your best ever shoot?" I slurred. Seriously, the vodka had gone straight to my head after only a couple of sips. I'd only had one glass of wine with dinner too. It must have been the late night, plus the long day affecting me. I was never usually a lightweight.

"Hmmm." He screwed up his face as if giving it serious thought. "Today? Because it meant I got to work with you."

"Smooth, very smooth." I tittered a laugh.

"Seriously. I haven't been offered many gigs lately. It's good to get some cash in. Things were getting tight."

His plight wasn't unusual, and I vaguely remembered him mentioning it when we'd first arrived that morning. Our business thrived on its fickleness. Luckily, I had a classic look, which led to a range of possible offers. Many times, I counted my genetic blessings.

"Do you want another drink?"

I squinted at my glass, already empty. How had that happened? It was still a little early to make my escape, so I agreed. While I waited for Mark to return, I pulled out my phone. The screen was blank, much to my disappointment. There was a part of me which had hoped Scott would message again. Although if I drank much more, I'd be the one giving him the booty call, not the other way around.

"Here you go." Mark placed another vodka and tonic in

front of me. "I got a double this time, hope that was okay?" He smiled, although it didn't quite reach his eyes.

"Mmm, great, thank you." I dropped my phone back into my bag, all thoughts of Scott forgotten. I reached for the glass, this time furnished with a straw and began to drink.

SCOTT

I'd done fuck all, all day. Unless you counted jerking off in the shower over Rosie Tatton. Again.

By the time late afternoon rolled around, I was bored as fuck.

Unless you counted the thirty minutes distraction after Rosie had sent me those lingerie shots and I then went on to search the internet for images of Victoria's Secret models.

When my phone pinged with a message, I leaped on it, wondering if Rosie had changed her mind.

Declan: fancy a beer?

The message was to the Trash Gun What's App group. Disappointment didn't even begin to cover it.

Mat and Bobby replied almost instantly in the affirmative.

The corner of my mouth curled up. We might have been out drinking into the early hours, but it didn't stop another session less than twenty-four hours later.

Scott: rude not to. The Bell in twenty?

A barrage of thumbs up emojis followed. We'd been going into the Bell since before we were recognised, and they could be relied upon to honour our need for privacy if required.

I dragged my sorry arse into my bedroom. Getting dressed hadn't been much of a priority until now, so I swapped my track pants and hoodie for black skinny jeans and a tight-fitting blue denim shirt. I added my usual rings and a pendant, then ran a hand through my hair. It wasn't like I was going out to impress someone.

As usual, I was the last to arrive. The lads had already commandeered our regular table in the corner.

"I'll get the first round," I announced.

"Second," said Mat, pointedly gesturing to the half empty pint glasses in front of the three of them.

"Whatever." I rolled my eyes and headed to the bar.

There was another guy waiting to be served. I stood next to him and patiently waited my turn. When the barman brought over his drinks - a pint and some kind of spirit with tonic - he handed over his card and slipped a hand in his pocket, pulling something out.

"What can I get you?" The second server appeared in front of me and all my attention transferred to her.

"Four beers, please." I passed her my credit card. "Can we start a tab? Table 14?"

She glanced at my name, then up at me. "Sure thing, Mr Lincoln. Do you want anything to eat?"

I bit back a comment about eating her out. She was new and far too young for me, possibly college age. "Not tonight, thanks." I smiled.

The guy next to me finally finished faffing with his drinks and pushed past me to get to his table. My gaze followed his path, landing on Rosie waiting at a table for him. I fought back the urge to go over to her. Now wasn't the time. The Ken doll must have been the guy from the shoot. My heart burned at the thought of him being so close to her. Especially when she had been wearing next to nothing. Jealousy was a bitch and I wasn't used to it.

"Here you go." The server slid the glasses towards me. "If you want any more, give me a wave and I can provide table service."

My dirty mind took her offer in completely the wrong way and I imagined her doing a table dance. I shook myself back to the present, politely said thank you and joined the others.

"Been a hell of a few weeks," said Declan, draining a large portion of his beer.

"Great tour, though," agreed Mat.

"If you don't count the arrest," added Bobby.

"Nothing to do with us. Total shit storm for Saff. She's been through a lot." I wasn't proud of my behaviour. Pretending we were an item when she was totally loved up with Tris hadn't been my best hour. I'd practically ruined their relationship. She had every right to hate me, yet despite everything which had happened between us, we had a strong friendship growing. Getting her to sing on the track had been a stroke of genius. Now we'd recorded it, it wouldn't be long before the song soared up the charts.

"What's next?" Mat leaned back in his chair. "There's

Wasted By My Side, but that's it. No new material. We've toured this album to death."

We signed a three-album deal with Numb Records and had the first album out and selling ridiculously well, but so far, we had nothing set in stone for the second. We did have some studio time booked, but currently nothing concrete to play in it. In the current climate, having a long break between album releases wouldn't be a good idea.

"We'll have new material," I said, confidently. "I'm going to my Mum's house after the Brixton gig. No stress, no pressure, see what inspo hits."

Mat sank a few mouthfuls of his pint. "And what about the rest of us?"

I shrugged. "Nothing stopping you working on stuff in preparation for our glorious return to the studio. I could do with a bit of a break, mate." I swirled the last of my pint around in my glass. "Caned it a bit hard on tour." It was only a slight understatement. Alcohol and cannabis were my main vices, although I'd also overindulged in coke. It was too easy to get hold of, and too effective at helping me maintain the high-intensity energy levels I needed to get through a gig.

Bobby and Declan nodded.

"Last thing we need is for you to end up in rehab. Didn't do Richey Mason any harm, though. Blood Stone Riot's new material is smoking." Declan made a gun gesture with his hand.

Our label mates were indeed making an impression, in the same way as us. We hadn't toured or played on the same bill as them, but maybe one day we would. Or maybe they could support us. It didn't hurt to think big.

Out of the corner of my eye, I spotted the guy Rosie was with approaching the bar again. Despite the server's extremely kind offer to provide waitress service, I leaped up.

"Another round?" I gathered the empty glasses up. "Shots?"

"Thought you were toning it down, Scott?" laughed Mat.

"Yeah, yeah, whatever." By the time I'd got to the bar, the guy had already been served and was putting the tonic into what I guessed was Rosie's glass. She didn't drink pints. I watched him slip a hand into his pocket and pull out a small bottle. Trying to mask his movements, he carefully shook a few drops into the glass and swished around the straw to mix it in.

"You okay, buddy?" he asked, finally noticing me observing him.

"What the fuck do you think you're doing?" I hissed, my tone low.

The little prick was about to give a spiked drink to Rosie.

"Sometimes they need a little encouragement." He winked. "Although you probably don't need any help with women, right, Scott?"

How dare he use my name like we were friends. I would never do what he was about to do. Not ever.

I nearly punched him. A reactive response. But, having seen what had happened to Saff's boyfriend recently, I didn't need the trouble violence would bring. Instead, I swiped the glass from the bar onto the floor. It landed with a crash, shattering on the tiled floor and spilling the contents in a puddle around the smashed glass.

Rosie's head whipped around at the sound, and she immediately spotted me. Her blue eyes appeared glassy, even from this distance.

How many drinks had he plied her with?

"You leave now. You never contact Rosie. You understand?" I jabbed my finger into his chest. "And you *never* do this to any woman ever again. Otherwise I will turn you in."

The guy's eyes bulged at my threats. "You don't even know who I am," he sneered.

"Yeah, I might not know now." I pointed in Rosie's direction. "But she does. And once I've told her what you've done, I'm sure she'll be more than happy to help me."

He backed off and hurried away, without a backwards glance. Sure he had gone, I went over to Rosie.

"Scott! What are you doing here?" She lolled back in her chair. I'd seen Rosie drunk before; this wasn't drunk.

"How many drinks have you had?"

Her eyes narrowed. "Why do you care? I was having a lovely evening with Mark."

Mark. I noted his name for future reference. "Tell me, Rosie."

She screwed up her face, as if working it out was difficult. "A glass of wine with dinner. God, it was awful. I mean, I'm into healthy eating and all that, but vegan food really is shit."

Needing her to focus, I bent down until I was eye level with her. "Concentrate, Rosie, it's important. How long have you been here? And how many drinks?"

"That was going to be my fourth, no, third, no…shit. I can't remember." She reached for her empty glass. "Mark was getting another one." She twisted and turned in her chair. "Where is he?"

"He's gone."

"Oh, we were having a nice evening." She pouted.

"Babe, you weren't. You just told me the restaurant was shit." I needed to get her out of there and back to her hotel where I could look after her properly.

"What are you doing here?" she asked again. Her hands snaked their way around my neck, pulling me closer to her, her fingers tangling in my pendant. "He was taking my mind off you, and now here you are."

Shit, now I knew she was more than drunk.

4

ROSIE

My vision swam and I blinked, trying to get Scott in focus. I didn't know why he was there, in the bar, and Mark had disappeared. He'd gone to get us more drinks.

Shit, how many had I had?

I stared at the table, trying to remember. There had been wine with dinner, then a couple of vodkas here. Or was it three? Normally, I'd be able to drink more than that without feeling woozy. I hadn't eaten much, even though the shoot had provided lunch and snacks throughout the day. Was it because I'd drunk last night as well? So many questions swirled around in my head. My fingers tangled in the leather thong of his pendant, hands snaking around the back of his neck.

"Where's Mark?"

Scott let out a hard breath. "He's gone. He won't be bothering you anymore."

I shook my head. "He wasn't bothering me tonight. We were... getting to know each other."

"Yeah, course you were. He wasn't spiking your drink to get in your knickers, he only wanted to 'get to know you better'." He put invisible air quotes around the end of the sentence. "Fucking prick."

He was doing what? I hadn't realised I'd spoken the question aloud until Scott responded.

"I watched him do it, Rosie. He said you needed a little encouragement." His mouth curled up into a sneer.

"I think I'm going to be sick." I pressed a hand to my mouth and stood up. My knees gave way beneath me, and I crumpled into Scott's arms.

He half-carried, half-walked me to the bathroom. When I suggested he let me go in there alone, he ignored my protests and strode through the door. I rushed into the cubicle and heaved, the vegan burger making a very unwelcome reappearance. Scott pushed in behind me, pulling my hair from my neck and holding it back out of the way as I retched again. His fingers stroked my back. Conflicted sensations flooded through me, a combination of horniness and comfort. I guessed part of that was to do with whatever Mark had given me. After a while, when I was sure there was nothing left to reappear, I sat back on my heels and wiped my mouth. A sticky sheen of sweat coated my skin. Why did it have to be Scott who was watching me vomit?

"Thank you for looking after me, Scott. I'll be okay now." I took several steadying breaths, trying to stop the waving crests of nausea.

"Like fuck you will be. I'll take you back to the hotel."

"I'll be fine," I protested. Embarrassment about him seeing me like this began to overtake my initial fizzle of attraction. My stomach swirled, and I managed to get my head over the toilet bowl just in time to threw up again. This time, I wasn't sure whether it was the drink or the drugs, or simply the hideousness of the whole situation.

"There is no way in hell I'm leaving you on your own tonight." He resumed the soothing circles on my back. "I'm not having you choke on your own vomit and die on me."

"Good to know," I managed.

The cycle of throwing up went on for a few minutes until I knew I wouldn't be sick again—nothing left to bring up either way. The thick-headed, woozy feeling remained though. I relented knowing Scott was right. I shouldn't be on my own. "Okay, you can walk me back to the hotel."

We left the cubicle, and I went to the sink to wash my face. There were two women touching up their make-up at the mirror. As we appeared, their mouths dropped, and their eyebrows raised.

"What are you doing in here? You're in that band," one demanded, pointing at Scott. "Did you two have sex in there?" Her nose wrinkled.

"Is that the only thing you think I'm capable of?" snapped Scott. "Don't know if you heard my friend throwing her guts up, which really doesn't do it for me by the way, but I wanted to make sure she was okay after some prick plied her with a date rape drug."

I shrank back against his chest, not wanting everyone to

know what had happened to me, how easily I'd been taken in by a guy who wanted to get into my pants. All I wanted was to go back to the hotel and hide under the duvet.

"Scott," I croaked. "Can we go now?"

"Are you okay?" the other woman asked. "Do you really want to leave with him?" She cast a side-eye glance in Scott's direction.

As he appeared to be the only one on my side right now, I definitely wanted to leave with him. "Yes. He really is a friend."

Ha. Lies. I didn't know what the hell we really were to each other, but I didn't think they'd accept fuck buddies as an explanation.

"If you're sure?" the first woman chimed in.

"I am." I took Scott's hand. "Thanks for looking out for me." I smiled at the two women as I dragged him out of the bathroom. "I'm sorry about them," I said, when we were in the main bar.

He shrugged. "People have an opinion. They think they know me."

I knew what he meant. Because we were both in the public eye, people thought they could make assumptions. Like Scott was the bad guy, we'd got it on in a public toilet— seriously, no, never—and he couldn't possibly be the one who had saved me.

Before we left, he took a diversion to a table in the corner where the other members of Trash Gun were nursing a round of drinks. Declan's brows shot up when he saw me.

"Rosie, I didn't know you were here." His gaze swung

between me and Scott, a questioning look in his eyes. "Scott didn't say anything."

"She wasn't here for me. She was with someone else." Scott slapped down a twenty pound note. "Get some more drinks in. I'll catch you later."

Mat gave me a knowing smile. "Oh, I get it."

"Why do you immediately think we're going to shag?" Scott's question came out harder that perhaps he intended.

"Because you've got history?"

I placed a hand on Scott's arm. "Leave it, Scott. Let's just go."

He huffed but did as I asked.

Silently, we walked along the road to the hotel. When we arrived in the foyer, I turned to him.

"Thank you for getting me back safely. I'll be fine on my own."

His green eyes narrowed. "I don't think so."

"Scott, seriously. All I need is a good night's sleep and some water."

"What if you get sick during the night? Who's going to be there to take care of you?"

I sensed he wasn't about to leave any time soon, so I had little option but to let him in. Without another word, I slipped the key card into the lift and pressed the button for my floor.

Once inside my room, I told Scott to make himself comfortable while I got changed. Inside the bathroom on my own, I examined my reflection in the mirror. I still looked like I'd drunk too much and the churning in my stomach didn't disagree. Despite feeling as if I could sleep standing up, I grabbed some cleansing wipes from the side, and scrubbed the remainder of my make-up from my face. A proper cleanse and tone routine would have to wait until the morning.

I stripped off all my clothes and dumped them in a ball in the corner of the bathroom. A shower seemed attractive, but so did sleep. The latter won out. I pulled on pyjama shorts and a vest top, taking the hotel bathrobe from a hook on the back of the door and securing the belt tightly around my waist. Finally, I wound my hair up into a messy bun.

With a deep breath aimed at calming my stomach, I exited the room.

Scott had made himself comfortable. He'd taken off his jacket and boots, and sprawled across the bed, his close-fitting denim shirt unbuttoned allowing me to get a delicious glimpse of his chest and tattoos. His gaze fixed on the television where some reality TV show played out. Hearing me close the bathroom door, his green gaze swung to me.

"Christ, you were ages. I thought I'd have to bang on the door if you didn't come out soon." He stretched his arms behind his head, the next button down on his shirt strained against his muscular chest.

I swallowed hard. *Stop those thoughts, Rosie. Nothing's going to happen tonight.*

Conflicted, I sank down onto the bed beside him, trying to stay as far away from him as I could.

He passed me a bottle of water from the mini-bar. "Here you go. Drink this."

Gratefully, I accepted. The water was delightfully cool

and soothed my sore throat and stomach. Despite my thirst, I tried not to down it all in one go.

"How are you feeling?"

"Like I've been on a bender with you for the last few days." I forced a smile. "Tell me it gets better."

He quirked a grin. "If you'd been on a bender with me, you'd know about it. And it never gets better, Rosie. Never."

5

SCOTT

Christ, she tested my willpower.

Normally, when we were in a hotel room— and it was always a hotel room—we were naked within seconds. I'd have her underneath me, on her knees, over the arm of the sofa, any which way.

Having Rosie a few feet away from me, wrapped in a hotel bathrobe, her hair pulled away from her gorgeous face, free of any make-up, made my dick twitch. Knowing I couldn't, shouldn't, touch her drove me crazy. I balled my hands into fists and crossed my arms, effectively stopping myself from reaching out for her. Nothing would have made me happier than gathering her into my arms to comfort her, and then...

I put a stop to those thoughts.

She'd been through a traumatic experience.

I was still up for tracking down that prick Mark and beating seven shades out of him. How many other women had he done the same thing to? Latent anger bubbled inside my chest. I shouldn't waste my energy on him, but I hated to think what might have happened if I hadn't seen what I did.

Rosie put the bottle of water she'd downed on the bedside table and turned to me. "Seriously, Scott, you don't have to stay. You've done so much already."

"I'm not leaving you alone. You might think you're okay, but what happens when you fall asleep?"

"I'll have some shitty, disturbed dreams because of whatever he gave me?"

"I don't want you to have shitty dreams." My fists clenched beneath my armpits.

"So because you're here, they'll be all rainbows and unicorns?" She glared at me. "I'll be fine."

"Jesus, just let me look after you!" I shifted into an upright position and fixed her with a similar stare. "Would that really be so bad?"

She folded her arms across her chest, causing her robe to fall to one side, allowing me a glimpse of her breasts. "Why, Scott? We're not in a relationship. You're not my boyfriend. You're not my anything."

Her words stung more than I expected.

Everything she said was true.

We hooked up.

We had sex.

We went on with our separate lives.

Until now, it had never been a problem.

Was she trying to say she wanted more from me?

I opened my mouth to challenge her, but she'd reached for the TV remote. Suddenly a rerun of Friends filled the room. Whatever conversation we'd been about to embark on was cut short by the image of Joey wearing all of Chandler's clothes.

Rosie sat up ramrod straight, her legs crossed in front of her, clutching the remote to her chest as if it were a weapon. Her gaze was fixed on the screen, although occasionally she reached for the water on the bedside table.

I attempted to engage her in conversation, pointing out things from the programme. She shut me down each time. Eventually I gave up.

We watched episode after episode, Rosie yawning more with each one. After a couple of hours, she finally fell asleep. The one good thing was she hadn't had to dash to the bathroom to be sick again. Hopefully it meant she felt better.

In her sleep, she turned and moved closer to me, snuggling up flush to my body. Her arm rested on my chest, a contented expression settling on her face.

Even if I wanted to, I couldn't move. I managed to reach for the remote and found a music video channel to keep me occupied. There was no way I would allow myself to fall asleep now. Even so, my eyelids drooped. I battled to stay awake. The robe Rosie wore moved as she did, those curvaceous breasts even more exposed than before. With a sigh, I pulled the garment up to protect her modesty.

A while later, the need to piss became more urgent and I wished I hadn't drunk so much beer. Carefully, I attempted to slide my body from next to Rosie without waking her. She muttered and groaned. I froze, expecting her to say something. When she turned over onto her other side and started to snore gently, I knew I was safe.

In the bathroom, I stared at my reflection in the mirror while I relieved myself. Dark circles ringed my eyes. It wasn't that I wasn't used to being up for hours at a time - I could easily go through the whole night without a wink of sleep with a little help from my white powdered friend - but the emotions which battled in my head wore me down.

A nightcap, albeit a late one, might help straighten me out.

Going back into the bedroom, I shoved my feet into my boots, found the key card for the room on the desk and slipped noiselessly from the room.

Sleep wasn't my friend at the best of times, with or without stimulants.

I was used to roaming around hotels in the early hours of the morning.

This hotel wasn't any different. A few night staff gathered in reception, chatting quietly or checking their phones.

"Everything okay, sir?" one of them asked as I headed for the front door.

"Yep, all good," I answered. "Nipping outside for a smoke."

"Sure." He nodded.

The street was quiet, save for the odd delivery truck or taxi. I pulled out my phone to see what time it was. Four a.m.

This time of day was my favourite. Watching the world come to life, giving that little bit of hope and optimism for the day ahead.

I sparked up a cigarette.

When I'd spoken to the rest of the band earlier, I had

been serious about wanting to get away and put down some new material. It would be the perfect chance to give my body a break, maybe even get into exercising more regularly in preparation for whatever tour would come our way next. Blowing out a stream of smoke, I coughed. Ha, maybe I could give up smoking as well.

It didn't take long to finish the cigarette. Given it was fucking freezing and I'd left my jacket in Rosie's room, it was no surprise. After I'd ground it out with my boot, I headed back inside.

"Can I get a drink?" I asked the same guy at reception I'd already spoken to.

"Sure, coffee, tea?"

"I was thinking more along the lines of a double whisky?"

His expression didn't change as he responded. "No problem. If you'd like to follow me."

My boots echoed on the tiled floor as I followed him across reception. He hadn't seemed phased by my early morning request for alcohol. This was obviously a hotel used to rock stars staying.

"What would you like?" he asked when we reached the bar.

"JD."

He gave me an imperceptible nod and turned away, sloshing a healthy double into a tumbler.

"Cash or card?"

Momentarily, I thought about charging it to Rosie's room. I wasn't that much of a prick though. Instead, I fished my phone from my pocket and tapped the card reader.

"Thank you. Let me know if you need anything else." Then he was gone, silently returning to his night-shift friends at reception.

I slumped onto one of the sofas and stretched my legs out in front of me. The unmistakable aroma of whisky invaded my nostrils. My thoughts turned to Rosie's earlier words. Was it possible she could be interested in something more than a hook-up with me? If so, what the fuck was she thinking? In the time we'd known each other, we'd never spent the night together, let alone woken up in the same bed. I always got out of there before that happened. Being that close to someone like Rosie Tatton wasn't me. It wasn't the Scott Lincoln I was. I preferred the uncomplicated nature of our unspoken relationship. The one which happened when and where we wanted it to, without any expectations or emotions. Or so I'd thought.

The protective feelings I'd had for her earlier came as a surprise. Sure, my cock loved her. I hadn't realised my heart might feel the same.

The alcohol burned as I slugged the whole glass in one go.

I deserved it for what I was about to do.

6

ROSIE

When I woke and stretched, the bedsheets next to me were cold.

My head pounded, and I honestly thought something had curled up and died in my mouth. I stared up at the ceiling, trying to process everything which had happened the previous evening. The shoot, Mark, the pub, Scott...

I sat bolt upright, gaze skimming the room from side to side. Where was he?

The bathroom door was open, the bedroom empty.

I was alone.

For a fleeting second, I thought Scott might have gone to get breakfast for us.

Then I caught sight of a piece of the hotel's notepaper poking out from underneath my phone. In spidery script, Scott had written *Had to go*.

Not even, 'I hope you're feeling better', or, 'sorry I had to go' or, 'see you soon'. Not even a kiss.

He'd done a runner.

I shouldn't have been surprised. It was a Scott Lincoln thing to do.

It would have been nice if he'd stayed until I'd woken up. Even checked to make sure I was okay. But why change the habit of a lifetime? Why not leave like he always did?

Cloaked in disenchantment, I hauled myself up and went into the bathroom, berating myself for booking such an early train. Although right now, I wanted nothing more than to be in my own home.

Relief settled over me as I entered my Notting Hill mews house less than three hours later. My sanctuary away from all the hustle and bustle of real life.

I got changed into a pair of yoga pants and a hoodie and then unpacked, chucking a load of washing on - yes, even supermodels wash their own knickers sometimes. Eventually, I settled on the sofa with no intention of moving.

I fired up my laptop, ready to check in on emails, when my phone rang. Hoping it would be Scott, I pounced on it, disappointed to see Saff's name flashing on the screen. My finger hovered over the accept button, debating whether to answer.

"Hi," I said.

"Oh, you are there! Thought you might have succumbed to Scott's charms again."

If only I had...then maybe last night wouldn't have happened.

"Don't be ridiculous. He's probably with that woman from the other night." I bluffed, hoping she wouldn't see through me. I hadn't told her about our latest hook up.

"And if he is, you've only got yourself to blame." Saff

huffed. "Honestly, you either need to kick him to the curb completely or marry the guy."

Given his behaviour this morning, the former certainly held more appeal. He definitely wasn't marriage material.

"Anyway, did you get home okay? How was your shoot? Did you see Ellie?" She changed the subject.

"Yes. Fine. And yes." Too tired to elaborate further, one words answers would have to do.

My short answers were clearly cause for concern. Saff proceeded to quiz me about every aspect of the *SFU* session. Before she could question me any further, I cut her off.

"Are you supposed to be doing something else? Like writing music? You don't usually get this hyper about my shoots."

"Damn, busted. Yeah, Darren wants to go back in the studio soon and I've promised him three new songs. Procrastination at its finest." She laughed. "No wonder you're my best friend if you can read me like that."

"I remember what you were like when we were trying to do homework."

"Nothing's changed." There was a pause as she shouted at someone in the background, presumably Tris, to say yes to a cup of tea. "By the way, are you coming to Brixton this Friday?"

"What's in Brixton?"

"Trash Gun have a support slot at the Academy. Scott's asked me to come and sing with them again. Tris is going back to his aunt and uncle's for some family thing, so I'll be on my own. I was going to say no, but it's good publicity and

Jonas thinks it's a brilliant idea." I could almost hear her rolling her eyes.

"This Friday?" I stalled on giving her a firm decision.

"Please, Rosie? I know I spent pretty much the whole time on tour alone with them recently, but it would be great if you could make it."

Saff wasn't usually one to beg.

"Can I see how I feel on Friday? I'm not sure what other work I'll be doing between now and then." Part of that was true, I couldn't remember what appointments I had or what castings were coming up.

A heavy sigh came down the line. "Yeah, I guess. But let me know soon, yeah?"

"Promise."

We chatted for a few more minutes before Tris came through with the tea.

"Gotta go, Rosie. See you Friday?"

"I guess…" I tried to up the enthusiasm levels in my tone, with little success. I ended the call and turned my attention back to my emails.

There was the usual plethora of newsletter updates, online shopping offers, requests for collaborations and so on.

My booker at the model agency reminded me of the casting I had on Monday. Normally, I didn't need to do castings as I sorted out a lot of collaborations myself. But this was for *Aspire* magazine's fashion spreads, and they didn't deal direct. The glossy fortnightly magazine was one of the very few I interacted with, and it had been a staple of my life for several years. The great mix of celebrity, fashion, style and music rivalled other publications such as *Grazia* or *Hello*. It would be a coup to land the job. I'd need to spend the weekend on virtual lockdown, making sure I ate clean and healthy, and absolutely *no* alcohol. It would be a great excuse as to why I wouldn't be able to go to the gig with Saff.

Ellie had sent through some more photographs from the shoot. I scrolled through them, some of which featured me and Mark laughing and giggling together, his hands on my skin. Nausea rose in my throat. Even thinking about what could have happened, if Scott hadn't arrived when he did, caused a mixture of anger and fear to bubble up.

How could I tell her what he'd tried to do?

At least we were unlikely to work together in the near future. He was one bad apple. Not everyone was like him.

I whiled away the afternoon replying to messages, and even posted a couple of the new *SFU* shots on social media, with some strategically placed teaser boxes so the whole look wasn't showing. I'd learned a long time ago brands didn't like you sharing their new content before they did. Ellie had given a date for the formal reveal. Of course, Scott had got an early preview.

Damn, there he was in my thoughts again.

Should I contact him? Thank him for looking after me? I didn't remember doing that at the time. Stalling, I went into the kitchen and faffed around making a cup of tea and finding some chocolate in the fridge to snack on.

Returning to the sofa, I started a message.

Rosie: Hey, hope you got home okay? Wanted to say thanks for looking after me last night. You were amazing xxx

Ugh. Too much.

Rosie: Hey, thanks for looking after me last night. Couldn't have got through it without you. See you soon xx

Fuck, seriously, Rosie.

Rosie: Thanks for looking after me last night x

Before I could change my mind, I pressed send. Like some kind of stalker, I stared at the screen, waiting to see if Scott had seen the message. Or whether I'd see the jumping dots which would tell me he was going to respond. Neither happened.

I tossed the phone to one side and switched on the TV instead. The channel showed *Friends*. A vague recollection of watching the show with Scott the previous evening swam into my head.

What made me think he'd immediately jump on something from me? We rarely contacted each other outside of the odd booty call. Why did I expect anything different today? Had there been some kind of magic shit in the stuff Mark had plied me with so that now I thought Scott was into me? My saviour?

There was no way I was going to his gig on Friday, no matter how hard Saff begged me.

7

SCOTT

Brixton was epic.

Totally fucking epic.

From the minute we arrived, they treated us like rock royalty. The headline act allowed us to watch their soundcheck before we did ours. Some of the notes the lead vocalist hit were ones I could only dream of. When I got into the studio again, I vowed to practice so I could become that good. Not that I wasn't, of course. The little pick-me-up I'd had before leaving the hotel convinced me I was invincible, the best thing ever. Nothing could bring me down.

Until I clocked Rosie.

I shouldn't have been surprised she was here with Saff.

Friends supported each other.

Friends didn't run out of a hotel room in the early hours of the morning.

Me and Rosie weren't friends.

My mood already enhanced with coke, spiked all over the place. One minute, everything was fine. No-one could damage the bubble around me. Next, I snarled at anyone who came within a five-foot radius.

Saff bore the brunt of it during our soundcheck. I yelled at her for screwing up the bridge in *Wasted By My Side*, when in reality it was nothing but perfection.

"Don't be a prick, Scott. You know it was fine," she spat back.

"I don't want fine, I want exceptional. Emotion, desire, longing." With each word, I wrung my hands.

"You should try some of those things yourself." Saff turned her back and stalked towards Declan. They whispered to each other, and Saff glanced over to the wings where Rosie watched from.

Every one of those emotions coursed through my body when I saw her. I shut them down. I had a performance to give.

"Shall we give it one more go?" asked Declan, ever the peacemaker. He adjusted his guitar and played the riff.

I shrugged. "If we think we can get it right this time." My grip tightened around the mic, gaze dropping to the floor as I prowled around the stage. Anything to avoid looking at Rosie.

Since the night I'd gone to her rescue, I'd blanked her. Leaving her a note was a bastard thing to do, and I hadn't replied to her message either. It had been almost a week. But seeing her tonight, all dolled up in a burgundy patterned dress which clung to every one of her curves, blonde hair pulled up into a messy kind of Brigette Bardot style, challenged my willpower again.

It would be so easy to hook up again.

We had all the classic signposts: we were at a gig; I was fucked up on coke. All it would take would be a few drinks... my hotel wasn't far away.

But I wasn't anything to her, she'd made that perfectly clear.

All the bad energy darting around my bloodstream had to be channelled in a different direction preferably into the best performance I'd ever done.

My head snapped up and I flexed my shoulders. I turned to Bobby behind the drums. "Ready?" I yelled.

Bobby raised his drumsticks in the air. "One... two... three..."

The cacophony of sound filled the empty Academy, bouncing off the walls with vehemence - mirroring my own emotions.

When it came to the bridge, I poured everything I had into the words, riffing off Saff, Declan and Mat. I spun around the stage, covering almost every inch, wanting to tire myself out, to bring myself back to an equilibrium.

Not once did I look to see if Rosie saw me.

Once we'd finished, Declan looked over at me, eyebrows raised. "You think we got it down okay this time?"

Sweat trickled down my back, and I caught my breath. "Might need to up it a notch for the real show."

Which was exactly what I did, after upping the chemical level in my bloodstream.

The entire thirty-five-minute set was as intense as any we'd done on tour. Condensing our setlist to that length had been the first challenge. Five, plus *Wasted*. It wasn't that I was bored of our songs, just that the time had come for new ones. While I knew the others were also working on tunes and lyrics, I couldn't wait to get away, get some quiet time and pour all my creative energy into fresh material.

The audience exploded as the final chords of *Wasted* abated.

A rush of being absolutely fucking adored hit hard.

The whole of the front row in the mosh pit went mental.

They wanted me.

I threw my arms up, mic clenched in one hand like a weapon.

"Thank you, Brixton!"

Screams and cheers echoed in my ears as I left the stage. I tossed the mic to one of the sound techs, and headed back to our dressing room, an oasis of calm amongst a veritable storm.

The four of us gathered together in the centre of the room, almost in a hot and sweaty group hug. The closeness I had with these guys was incredible. Ten years of being together, and it still felt as raw and natural as the early days.

A few moments of quiet reflection and we broke apart, high fiving each other.

"You staying around for the rest of the night?" Declan asked.

We'd been provided with all access passes for the head-line set. Much as I liked the opportunity we'd had to support, I wasn't so keen on the band's music.

"Me and Rosie are going to get a late dinner, if you want to come with us?"

I'd almost forgotten Saff was still there.

What a choice.

It would be so easy to say yes to Saff. To go out and pretend everything was fine between me and Rosie.

But it wasn't, and I didn't have the first clue how to fix it.

Talking to her would be the obvious start.

I didn't do obvious.

"Nah, not tonight. Don't want to kill the adrenaline buzz."

"I'm sure Rosie would be delighted for you to describe her like that." Saff shook her head. "Whatever, man." She approached me, already changed out of her stage clothes, and kissed me on both cheeks. "I'll see you soon. Stay in touch."

Potentially, I wouldn't see her for a while. We had no other gigs in the diary, and no plans to work together again. I'd miss her. While I'd been a total arse to her on tour, she had her moments, and we understood each other. She was also the one link I had to Rosie, if I didn't see her then that link would be broken.

I was undecided as to whether it was a good thing.

Declan, Mat and Bobby went off to watch the band, leaving me alone.

Bad move.

I checked my jacket to see if there was any coke left. If I had been true to form, there would be, and I wasn't disappointed. I snorted the remaining couple of lines and wiped the remnants of the powder into my gums. Fuck, I loved that initial rush.

Still dressed in stage clothes, dark skinny jeans, boots, and a tight-fitting black t-shirt, I exited the dressing room, in search of something. Or someone. I hadn't quite decided yet.

The sound from the stage drew me to where everyone else watched from.

I spotted a hot looking redhead, wearing cut-off denim shorts and a tight-fitting lacy black top, standing in the wings and sidled up beside her. My mouth curled up at one corner. It was someone, not something, I needed.

"Hey," I whispered-shouted into her ear.

She turned, eyeing me blankly. "Um, hi?"

"You enjoying the music?" Lame, but it was all I had.

Her eyes lit up. "Yeah, they're great. Have you seen them before?"

I sucked in a breath. Clearly, she had no idea who the hell I was—disheartening. "A few times," I lied. "Did you watch the support act?"

"Only got here a little while ago. I can't believe I got backstage!" She waved the lanyard at me.

My gaze travelled over her body. I could. She had every-thing to get her the all access pass. "I can show you around, if you like?"

She flicked her head around to mine. "Oh, I was going to wait until they'd finished and then see?" Her finger gestured to the band onstage.

Clearly uninterested, she turned her attention back to the performance.

For a moment, I considered pushing it. Then realised I'd be like that prick Mark who tried to take advantage of Rosie. And I would never - ever - do that to a woman. Not bothering to say hi to Declan, Mat and Bobby, I slipped away back to the dressing room.

I found my phone and fired off a quick message to one of my contacts. Seconds later the notification pinged.

Something would have to do instead.

8

ROSIE

W atching Scott perform gave me all the feels. And I mean *all* of them.

Sure, I'd seen the band at the launch party only a few days ago, but this was next level.

He prowled around the stage like he owned it, connecting with audience members intimately, as if they were the only two people in the room. At one point, he cast a look into the wings where I stood, his grey eyes like flints as they bored into mine. I swear a spontaneous orgasm ripped through me from his intense gaze.

I bit my lip as he turned away, launching into another song and performance to go with it.

It was torture.

He hadn't replied to my last message. I didn't want to come across as all needy-stalker and send another one. I'd finally agreed to come tonight late this afternoon. Having debated with myself for the past few days, I decided I wanted to be here for Saff. Not for Scott.

Ha, who was I trying to kid?

"I asked him if he wanted to come for dinner." Saff stood in the restroom, reapplying her lipstick, while I waited for her.

I could pretend I didn't know who she was talking about, but there was no point. "And?"

"Said he was going to stay and watch the headline band." She pursed her lips together, then touched up the smudge in her cupid's bow.

Figured as much. There would be more fresh meat for him there, rather than hanging out with me and Saff.

I couldn't shake the feeling he was pissed at me.

But then I also couldn't shake why it bothered me so much.

"Come on, let's go eat. I'm starving." Saff turned away from the mirror, fixing me with a grin.

We ended up in a burger place not far from the venue. A small part of me hoped Scott might change his mind and join us. As I didn't have a casting until Monday, I chose a cheeseburger and chips, plus wine. I could be more sensible over the weekend. I'd live on water and celery if I had to. Saff ended up ordering the same, after taking an age looking at the menu, and changing her mind about five times. I pitied Tris when he took her out, her indecisiveness was legendary.

"What's going on with you and Scott then?" Saff got straight to the point once our drinks arrived. She was nothing if not direct.

I shrugged, unsure how to answer.

"I saw you giving him the eye at The Matchbox, did you hook up after?"

I chewed on an olive and nodded.

"Oh, Rosie." Saff let out a sigh. "I never know whether to be disappointed in you or angry for you."

The waiter appeared with our food and we paused the conversation while he set down the plates.

"What do you mean?" I asked, shaking vinegar over my chips.

"You and Scott, all this on/off stuff. You can do so much better than him."

I vaguely recalled having a similar conversation with her after she'd been papped with a married footballer. Had Saff listened to me? Of course not. Did that mean I should listen to her?

Saff stuffed a forkful of chips into her mouth. "We need to find you a nice guy," she mumbled.

"Why?" I pulled a face.

She directed a finger at her chest. "Case in point. Look what happened when I stopped hanging around with the likes of Troy Carson or Carl Doherty."

I considered her justification. True, when she started seeing Tris it had been for show, to get her out of trouble with her cousin, the record company and the gossip columns. Then as they grew closer, she had softened, and fallen in love with him. As a painter and decorator working for his uncle, he was a grafter, working hard for everything he had. Basically, the polar opposite of Saff, the wild child, rock star who didn't like obeying the rules. Or at least she had been. Since they'd moved in together, she had lost some of her hard edginess. Not angry at the world all the time she stopped doing things simply to piss off her cousin. I loved both versions of her, although this new, sentimental side of her was a revelation.

"Yeah, I get it." I sipped my wine, pretending to give her suggestion some serious thought. "But where do I find the good ones?"

Excited that her suggestion might actually have sunk in, Saff waved her fork at me. "I bet Tris has some friends from back home. I can speak to him and see who he thinks might be a suitable match."

I gulped. I hadn't expected her to move things on quite so quick. Let's not get carried away.

"We can arrange a double date, dinner at ours. A sort of housewarming party!"

"Um. Okay?" I hesitated. Much as I loved Tris and how he'd changed Saff, I wasn't sure a manual labourer would quite do it for me. Or was I being too judgemental?

"We'll arrange it soon. I'm meant to be doing some stuff with the guys in the studio. Promised Jonas we'd have the second album sorted by now." She rolled her eyes. "It's like running through treacle, none of us are inspired."

"Do you think you'll go back out on tour again?"

She contemplated the question. "Given the mess we got into with Trash Gun, I think we'll be looking to do something low key, maybe on our own. I can't see Jonas rushing us back into high profile stuff, let alone the record company. And I don't need them freaking out again."

"What about if Scott wanted you to support them?" I don't know why I felt compelled to bring him up again. It was almost as if should I stop talking about him, he wouldn't exist.

"Nah, I think that ship's sailed. We got all the publicity around *Wasted By My Side* done, it's been released now. There's nothing else to do now except watch the royalties roll in." Saff laughed. "Ironic I'll probably make as much from that collaboration as I would with TheSB."

We decided to share a dessert and carried on chatting shit for another hour. It wasn't often we got to have gossip filled, girlie nights out and I was grateful for the distraction.

It was shortly after midnight when I finally rolled into my house.

I flopped down onto the sofa and switched on the television, flipping through the music channels until I found something to hold my attention.

When the original version of *Wasted By My Side* came on, I was transfixed, unable to tear my eyes off the screen. A younger version of Scott filled the picture, his mouth forming the words of the song. I turned up the volume, his voice blowing up the room. Lost in the moment, I stared at him, wishing I knew where we really stood.

9

SCOTT

After the headliners had finished playing, they invited me to an afterparty, which began in the dressing room. Their rider was spectacularly loaded with beer, whisky, weed, coke. Whoever had sorted them out had done a great job.

I helped myself to whisky and a joint and then slumped down on one of the low sofas against the wall. Fishing a lighter from my pocket, I lit the joint and observed the activity around me, blowing a plume of smoke up into the air.

Trash Gun after parties had a tendency to get out of control, but this was another level. The band, much harder and with more metal bias than us, clearly had a different class of fan. Out of the corner of my eye, I clocked the lead singer with a Sharpie signing the enormous tits of a bleached blonde.

"You hanging around long?" A black-haired woman, all curves and excess make-up, sidled over to me and sat down beside me. And when I say next to me, I actually mean practically in my lap. She sipped seductively from a bottle of beer, watching me through hooded lids.

"Probably." I shrugged. "Nowhere else to be."

Her mouth curved into a smile. "Good to know. I saw your set earlier. Very impressive." Her gaze moved between my legs, an eyebrow arching.

I sucked in a breath. Was this what I really wanted? A one nighter with someone who only seemed interested in one thing? I squeezed my eyes shut. It was my usual modus operandi, who was I to judge?

"Hey, Scott." Mat's voice broke through the white noise in the room.

My eyelids flew open to see his look of disapproval at my current state.

"We're heading off. Are you coming?" His eyes flicked between me and the woman.

She gripped my thigh. Her fingers, topped with particularly dangerous looking nails, edged their way towards my crotch. I shifted uncomfortably, not wanting Mat to witness what might happen next. I grasped her wrist, stopping whatever she was about to do, not needing an audience.

"Nah, I think I'm going to stay here a bit longer." I exhaled in his direction, watching his nose wrinkle at the smell. "Catch you later, yeah?"

"Be careful, Scott." His tone had a hard edge. "Make sure you don't end up in the gossip columns again."

My hand grazed the base of the woman's spine. "You got it. I'm sure I can find someone to keep me on the straight and narrow."

The woman giggled and adjusted her position, almost straddling me.

Mat huffed, his eyes narrowing as the scene unfolded in front of him. "Whatever," he sighed, before turning on his heel and stalking out of the room.

"Who was that? Your minder?"

If she really had watched the set earlier, she would have known Mat was the one dropping the bass lines to our songs. Unless, of course, she only had eyes for me. I laughed out loud.

"What's your name?" I asked. If she was going to suck my dick at some point that night, I felt I ought to know.

"Talia."

"Well, Talia, do you want to get out of here?"

Talia glanced around the room. "Why would we want to leave? There's everything I could possibly want here, booze, weed, you..." Her body ground against mine; my dick grew hard.

While she had a point, I didn't make a habit of public displays of affection and I certainly had no intention of screwing Talia with an audience. The only thing I wanted an audience for were my gigs.

"Then let's get some more drinks and another joint." I ground out the remains of my first with the heel of my boot.

"You got it."

Talia lifted herself off me and sashayed across the room, tossing her black hair. I watched the swing of her hips, admiring the curve of her arse. She could make the perfect distraction.

My phone vibrated in my pocket. Normally, I would

ignore it, but something made me look at the message. When I stared at the screen, I wish I hadn't.

Rosie: Great gig tonight, thought you were amazing, as ever. Sorry to have missed you after. Catch up soon? xxx

It was as if Manchester had never happened. I'd seen her around tonight, of course I had. And Saff had invited me out on their dinner date. But I couldn't sit and make polite conversation with Rosie Tatton. Not without wanting to strip every piece of clothing off her and explore every single inch of her creamy smooth skin. I scrolled back in the message to the pictures she'd accidentally sent me from her last shoot. Desire clutched at my chest. Fuck, she really was beautiful.

"Here you go." Talia thrust a tumbler of whisky under my nose. "Your girlfriend checking up on you?" She laughed.

I'd drunk enough to be on the verge of self-destruction.

Rosie wasn't here. Talia was.

I switched my phone off and shoved it in my pocket.

"I don't have a girlfriend."

With a wicked grin, I pulled Talia back into my lap.

There wasn't much of the evening I remembered after that.

Hazy flashbacks of several lines of coke, washed down with even more whisky. Laughing and joking with the lead singer of the headline band. Jamming with their guitarist. Generally causing mayhem until we got kicked out of the dressing room. The party continued at a basement bar close to the venue, which stayed open until the very early hours of the morning. I honestly didn't remember how much, or what, I'd drunk or taken. All I knew was that I wasn't feeling any pain.

When we were finally asked to leave the bar around four in the morning, Talia glued herself to my side. We fell out of the doors, stumbling around and trying to get our bearings. I had no idea where the hotel was or how the hell I would get back there.

Squinting, I spotted a guy with a long lens camera lurking around in one of the streets opposite.

"Oy!" I yelled. "What the fuck are you doing?"

"Leave him, he's not worth it," mumbled Talia, wobbling on her heels. "You're probably not the money shot anyway." She shoved me back against the wall, pressing her tits against my chest. "Come on, are we going back to your hotel?" Her breath smelled of beer and smoke, which did nothing for my senses.

My stomach heaved against the smell. I turned my face away, bent over and threw up, narrowly avoiding her shoes.

"Ugh, that's disgusting." She recoiled, putting some well-deserved distance between us.

"Think our night's over, Talia, don't you?" I slurred, wiping my mouth.

Her head snapped around to see the other members of the band heading down the road towards the taxi rank.

"Wait for me!" she called. Without another word in my direction, she tottered off after them, leaving me alone.

I slumped back against the wall, the cement rough through my shirt. I couldn't have felt worse if I'd tried.

Somehow, I managed to get back to the hotel and made it back to my room.

I stripped off my clothes and slid under the duvet, the white cotton cooling my heated skin.

The whole evening had been a fiasco. One glimmer of hope was I hadn't brought Talia back to the hotel. Shagging around when I was off my face was never a good idea.

I should have taken Saff up on her offer of dinner.

I should have left when Mat asked me to.

I should have left when Rosie messaged me.

The third realisation was the one which hit home.

Now all that was left was a heap of regret and a really nasty taste in my mouth. I wasn't even kidding. The sour taste of drink, drugs and vomit swirled around, making me retch again. I reached for one of the bottles of water which had thoughtfully been placed on the bedside table and gulped the whole thing down in one.

I unearthed my phone from the pile of clothes on the floor. Dead. Needed charging. Where the fuck was the charger? I focused on the room and spotted my bag on the floor by the wardrobe. I never bothered unpacking in hotels when we only stayed one night. Dragging my sorry arse across the room, I found the charger and plugged the phone in.

A flurry of messages pinged up on the screen. Mostly from the band's What's App group celebrating the success of our set, several from a number I didn't recognise - which I guessed may have been Talia, given the suggestive nature of the content, although it was entirely possible I'd given my number out to any number of women given the state I'd been in - and the usual ones from management after a gig.

Nothing more from the one person I wanted to hear from.

Switching the device to silent and leaving it across the room, well away from me, I slunk back to the bed and cocooned myself in the duvet.

Everything could wait.

Right now, I needed to sleep.

10

ROSIE

The *Aspire* casting took place at their offices off of Carnaby Street. I loved this part of London, always so vibrant and ever changing, which was why I'd got there early to grab a takeaway coffee and sit to watch the world go by for a while.

Idly, I read one of the gossip sites I infrequently checked for stories about myself. Indulgent? Narcissistic? Egotist? Probably. It wasn't something I did often, and also allowed me to check in on some of my friends and alert them to anything which looked dodgy. Saff, for instance. The minute I opened it up, my stomach sank.

The headline story featured Scott falling out of a club with a black-haired woman I didn't recognise. The date was from a couple of nights ago - the evening of the Brixton gig.

I shouldn't have been surprised, but I didn't expect the jealousy to burn quite as deep as it did.

I stared at the photograph. He looked wasted.

What was I doing?

He had plenty of opportunities to be with me that night, yet he'd chosen to turn them down and do his own thing.

He clearly wasn't interested in me.

With a sigh, I shut down the site and checked the time. Only a few minutes until the casting at *Aspire's* office, I headed to their building.

The reception was a light, airy space, similar to most other office buildings. Framed photographs of various front covers were hung up on the walls, cataloguing their most successful issues. Maybe one day I'd get my own cover.

"Hi, I'm here for the casting?" I said to the receptionist.

"Take a seat." She gestured to where two other girls were already waiting.

I never got used to seeing women so similar to me. The same blonde hair, similar height, build and weight. Obviously they wanted a certain look, and I wasn't the only one who had it. We nodded at each other as I sat down next to them. One of them definitely looked familiar and I'd been up against her for other jobs, which she'd ended up getting. Already, my chances seemed slim.

The woman I recognised as the magazine's fashion director approached me, resplendent in a pair of navy capri pants, a floaty, printed blouse in similar tones, and matching kitten heels.

"Hey, Rosie, good to meet you."

Fuck, I wished I'd made more of an effort. In comparison, my dark jeans and simple black t-shirt paired with a forest green blazer seemed uninspiring, dull even.

They were looking to cast for a vintage day-to-night

spread, and the fashion director had definitely got the message. I should have heeded it myself.

The casting followed the usual structure. I followed her to a meeting room where she flicked through my portfolio. Occasionally, she would stop on a particular shot and ask a few questions about the context. We chatted briefly about some of the brands I'd worked with, as well as finding out more about their ideas for their shoot. The whole thing lasted little longer than ten minutes.

She closed my portfolio and passed it back to me. "We're looking to have a couple of male models on the shoot," the fashion director said. "I've got one here now, if you're okay to have a couple of shots done?"

"Sure." I smiled. "Can't do it if there's no chemistry."

I walked behind her down a corridor into a small room, which was a cross between a fashion cupboard and a studio. Half was set up with a simple white backdrop and a camera, while the rest of it resembled my wardrobe, clothes bulging out of cupboards, accessories scattered around the available surfaces, and mismatched shoes on the floor.

"Can you wait here? I'll go and get him."

My magpie eyes scanned the various treasures while I waited. It was like heaven in there. Just as I was about to pick up a Balenciaga handbag, she came back.

"Rosie? This is Mark. We did an initial casting last week and he's in the running."

Mark.

Common name. There must have been hundreds of models called Mark. The chances of it being him were...

I turned, and as soon as I saw who was in the doorway my hand flew to my mouth.

"Rosie," he said. "Who knew we'd be up for the same job so soon after working together?"

I swallowed down the bile in my throat. *Keep calm, don't let him bother you, there's someone else here this time.*

"Are you okay?" the fashion director asked. "You've gone awfully pale."

"No, um, I'm fine," I lied. "We were on a shoot together last week for *SFU*."

"Ah, good. That means you've already got a good relationship if you've shot lingerie together." She clapped her hands together.

Mark's gaze raked over my body. I imagined him remembering me in the *SFU* bra and panties. I hated he knew what that looked like. I hated how he thought he could take advantage of me. I hated how he made me feel now.

I was a professional though, and despite my hatred of him, I had to get through these brief test shots and then get the hell out of there.

We were directed to our places in the studio half of the room. Naturally, we fell into poses without the need for further explanation. Even so, my body seemed unnaturally stiff as I tried to avoid Mark touching me. Knowing what he had wanted to do made my skin crawl and any time he got close, I pulled away sharply.

The fashion director snapped away, not saying a word. These shots couldn't be good. They'd be worse than the ones I did in my first ever casting. And we were well into four figures for those now.

Eventually after what felt like an hour, although in reality it was probably only around five minutes, she called a halt to proceedings.

"That's great, guys," she said, with a smile which didn't quite reach her eyes. "Rosie, I think that's all I need from you today. We'll be in touch soon if we want you to come back. And Mark, if you're happy to wait a little longer, I think there will be one more shoot."

"Sure, not a problem." Mark beamed. "I don't have anywhere to be."

One of the other members of the fashion team popped his head around the door and beckoned to the fashion director.

"Are you okay to see yourself out? I need to deal with something." She cast a look over her shoulder at me as she rushed away. "Good to meet you."

I wouldn't be seeing her again anytime soon. At least not if this casting had gone as badly as I thought. Relieved to be out of there, I stepped towards the doorway, only to have Mark grab my arm.

"I didn't think I would be seeing you again so soon either," he hissed in my ear. "Not after your rock star boyfriend threatened me."

"He's not my boyfriend." I twisted in his grasp, but he tightened his fingers around my forearm painfully.

"And he's not here now, either."

"As if you'd be stupid enough to try anything." I clung on to that thought.

Mark's other hand trailed a path across my breasts, sliding underneath my blazer and squeezing my right tit hard. I winced, trying to pull away from him, but his other arm encircled me.

"I thought we'd been getting on so well."

"So well that you needed to *drug me* to get me to sleep with you." I struggled to get out of his grasp. "How many other women have you done that to, Mark? Huh? Or was I the first?"

"Women like you never look at guys like me." His face was twisted into a mask. "I'm the prop at the side, never the one you'd really be interested in. You're too busy making love to the camera. Don't think I didn't notice the looks you were shooting towards the photographer. Thinking about *him,* were you?" He pushed himself towards me again, his nose only inches from mine.

"What if I was? Why did it give you the right to spike me?" My voice came out louder than I anticipated; the words reverberated around the room.

"What's going on in here? Rosie? Mark?" The fashion director reappeared, taking in the scene in front of her: me cowering away from Mark, him towering over me.

Instantly, he released my arm. I let out a breath, not realising I'd been holding it in all this time.

Silence descended. I waited for Mark to explain, but he wasn't forthcoming.

Anger overtook any fear I had.

I drew back my shoulders and stood tall. "I'd like to thank you for the opportunity today, but I'm afraid if you're planning to work with Mark, you won't be working with me." Without saying another word, I grabbed my bag and walked out.

I pushed open the door to the outside world and gulped in deep breaths of air.

There was only one person I needed to speak to right now.

I pulled out my phone and dialled his number.

11

SCOTT

Day one at the family bolthole, and I hadn't yet managed to get out of bed, whiling away the time watching some weekday morning magazine programme. Truth be told, I'd always had a crush on the blonde presenter.

Friday night slash Saturday morning's excesses finally took their roll. I had slept way past check out time yesterday. Mat had almost broken the door down, thinking I'd done something stupid, until one of the housekeeping staff let him in. Then he yelled at me for a good twenty minutes, calling me every name under the sun. Didn't bode well for us spending the journey home cooped up in a confined space.

The journey back to Manchester had been silent.

A traffic jam on the motorway meant we were on the road for close to five and a half hours. Tempers were frayed by the time I got dropped off. The wordless disapproval from Mat, Declan and Bobby couldn't have been more apparent.

I got into my flat, dumped my bag and fell straight into bed again.

An insistent buzzing on the intercom roused me around midday on Sunday. Shaking the fog from my brain, I remembered I'd organised a car for the week in the Cheshire countryside. Pulling on some clothes and shoes, I did all the necessary checks with the drop off driver, signed my life away and took possession of the keys for the Range Rover. The temptation to go back to bed was a strong one, but I stopped myself. If I got my shit together, I could get to the house late afternoon and then finally relax.

Which is exactly what I did.

My phone rang. I ignored it. No-one was meant to be bothering me here. Not even the band.

Not bothering to even look at who was calling, I let it go to voicemail. If it was important, they'd leave a message, or call again.

The duvet enveloped me in warmth and comfort. I needed a break; an enforced detox. The craziness of the tour, plus the way I reacted at the Brixton gig meant I'd put more bad shit into my bloodstream than was good for any man.

I needed quiet calm and no distractions.

The phone chirruped again, this time with a message.

Seriously, could people not leave me alone?

Reluctantly, I reached for the device, having every intention of switching it off until I saw who had sent it.

Rosie: Scott, can you call me? I really need you...

The message was enough to spark me into life. A voice-mail flashed up with her name. I sat bolt upright and dialled voicemail.

"Scott? It's me, Rosie. I...I've just been to a casting for a job and... well, Mark was there. He threatened me again and... I...I don't know what to do. Can you call me back? Please?"

The way her voice cracked on the last word almost had me reaching through the phone to grab her and bring her here. What had that fucker done this time? Hadn't I been clear he wasn't to contact her again? I did as she asked and called.

She answered immediately. "Oh, thank God," she said, her voice breathy.

"Where are you?" I demanded.

"Carnaby Street. *Aspire* had a casting and I didn't know they were going to do chemistry shots and when I went into the room it was him and I didn't know how to react because I really wanted the job..."

"Shhh, calm down." I cut her off as she babbled down the line at me. "Is he with you?"

"No, I left before he had a chance to follow me."

"So you're in a public place where he can't find you?"

"Yes. I planned to head straight home."

"Good. Do that."

"Should I report him? God, what if I bump into him again?" Her voice went up an octave.

What possessed me to make the offer I did, I would never know. It seemed like the right thing to do. "You won't. Pack a bag, get on a train and come join me here."

"In Manchester?" she asked.

"I'm not at home, but I'll tell you where I am. Gonna be here for the week to chill, and I want to start making new music." I paused. "Sounds like you need to do something similar?"

The silence which met my suggestion was an answer in itself. She would turn me down gracefully, thanking me for the offer, and promise me she'd get Saff and Tris to look after her.

Never in a million years did I expect her to say, "Can you message me the details? And will you be at the station?"

My jaw dropped. It was a good thing we weren't on a video call.

"You'd really come here? Rosie, are you sure?"

"Are you backtracking on your offer, Mr Lincoln?"

Her tone caused the hairs on the back of my neck to raise. "Never."

"Then I'll see you at the station."

The line went dead. I stared at the blank screen unable to believe what had just happened.

Rosie Tatton was coming to spend the week with me.

First, to get cleaned up. I hauled my body out of bed and padded into the bathroom.

There was a huge shower in one corner, more than big enough for two, with a waterfall shower head. I turned the water on and let it cascade over my head. The flow and temperature soon soothed my bones.

What the hell was I going to do with Rosie for an entire week?

Several thoughts ran through my brain, causing my dick

to harden. Tempting though it was to bring some much-needed relief, I resisted. If Rosie was up for some of our usual no-strings sex, it wouldn't be a bad thing. There would be no pushing it though; she was still vulnerable after her latest encounter with that Mark guy.

Blasting the water to cold, I shivered for the last minute of my shower, before stepping out and towelling off to pull some clothes on.

For once, I made my bed, then went to check on one of the guest bedrooms. Smaller than mine, it still held a king-sized bed and the cool blue decor instilled a sense of calm. It should suit Rosie perfectly.

Downstairs in the kitchen, I opened the fridge and stared at the empty shelves. I wished I'd had the foresight to sort out an online shopping delivery. My stomach rumbled. I'd give my right arm for a bacon sandwich.

Rosie wouldn't arrive for at least three hours. I had plenty of time to sort out supplies and satisfy my hunger.

I grabbed the keys to the Range Rover from off the side and headed out. The centre of the village was only a five-minute drive from the house, one I could have easily walked, but with shopping on my mind, staggering back with bags full of stuff wasn't really an option. The vehicle stood out like a sore thumb amongst the small, practical cars in the car park. Aiming the fob at the door, I locked it and went to the cafe I usually frequented when I was there.

"Hello, what can I get you?" The teenage girl behind the counter regarded me with a mixture of curiosity and interest. From the way her demeanour changed, I guessed she recognised me.

"Bacon sandwich and a black coffee, please. Large, if possible." I treated her to a wide smile.

She stifled a giggle, before turning away and shouting my order into the kitchen.

Resisting the urge to roll my eyes, I left her some money on the counter, and sat down at a table in the corner.

Scott: How's the journey going?

I debated adding a kiss but then thought better of it and pressed send.

Rosie: Running late. Left London about twenty minutes ago.

Scott: No worries. Let me know when you're about half an hour away? I'll be at the station.

Rosie: Sure. It is too early for a drink?

Scott: Never! Don't arrive pissed though…lol

A drunk Rosie wouldn't be good at all, even though with all the upheaval of the day, she probably deserved something to take away the stress.

Rosie: Promise. Wait, the trolley's coming…I'll be in touch later xx

The waitress arrived with my breakfast - if you could call it that at one thirty in the afternoon. "Here you go. I brought your change too."

I waved her away. "No need. Put it in the tips jar."

Her cheeks pinked. "Wow, that's really kind of you." She took the ten pound note and odd change from the plate with my receipt on, then walked away.

Half an hour later, my tummy full of delicious smoked, salty bacon and white bread, I ventured into the supermarket. Mundane chores such as this were something I didn't usually have to deal with. Online deliveries were my way of surviving. Either from the supermarket themselves or from local takeaways. Actual shopping was a total novelty. I pushed a trolley around the aisles, throwing in various items which looked interesting or I liked, giving some consideration to things Rosie might want. Having never really spent time with her over a meal, I had no idea if she was into healthy food, was vegan, vegetarian or had a peanut allergy. Taking every possible eventuality into consideration, I ended up spending over two hundred and fifty pounds. Although looking at the bottles of beer and wine, a pretty healthy amount of that had gone on alcohol. I piled the bags into the back and drove back to the house.

After I'd unpacked, I still had some time to kill before Rosie arrived. I headed downstairs to the cellar. It had been converted into a games room slash chill out area, with comfy sofas, a massive TV screen and a pool table. I opened up the case of my acoustic and settled down on one of the sofas. I wasn't as adept at playing as Declan, although the majority of our material started off with me coming up with a shitty riff and some kick ass lyrics, which the others would help mould into something amazing. With my current mindset, I wasn't entirely sure what was going to come up, but I had to try. My fingers slid over the fretboard, picking at the strings, and I lost myself in the creative process.

12

ROSIE

Thankfully, the woman and her three kids who I'd been sharing the table got off the train before me. Normally, I was a patient woman, but spending the past two hours with one child kicking me in the shins, and the other screaming in my ear that he was hungry, had seriously tested my kindness. I didn't want to be the judgy woman who thought the mother couldn't cope, but clearly the poor woman was exhausted.

When the train manager appeared with the trolley, I seriously considered ignoring Scott's warning about getting drunk and buying up the entire stock of alcohol. Instead, I kindly offered to buy snacks for the family, a false smile plastered on my face.

"Oh my goodness, that's so kind of you! You didn't have to do that." The mother babbled. "I'm so sorry about Finley's behaviour, he's not normally so loud, but he's been a bit under the weather this week."

Watching her young son stuff the sandwich into his mouth practically whole, made me wonder how ill he'd actually been.

I resisted the urge for a gin and tonic, and instead got a juice and a chicken salad sandwich. At least that's what the label said, although it could have been cardboard and cotton wool.

Scott's offer had come out of left field.

We'd never spent the night together. Yet here we were about to spend however many days in each other's company, twenty-four hours a day.

Nerves bubbled in my stomach. I couldn't deny the prospect of finding out if there was anything more than simply the physical between us was attractive.

I pulled my phone out. Gah, no signal. I tapped my fingernails on the edge of the table. If I couldn't let Scott know I was almost there, how would I get back to his house?

"We're coming into a station now," the train manager said, noticing my apparent agitation. "You'll be able to get signal there."

"Thank you." I smiled. "I need to let my, um, friend know where I am."

"Where are you staying?"

I pulled in my bottom lip. "I don't actually know. It's his family house or something." I found the message with the address and showed it to him. "This is it."

The train manager let out a low whistle. "Not a bad place at all. Lovely village, got a good pub. Make sure you go to the Kings Arms, they do a mean pie in there." One of his colleagues waved from the other end of the coach, and he trotted off, ready to prepare for coming into the next station.

The promised 4G signal appeared, and I fired off a message to Scott to tell him where I was. The next station, in around half an hour's time, would be where I got off.

Over the course of the next thirty minutes, I touched up my make-up, pulled a comb through my hair and practised a neutral facial expression.

The station was the cutest little picture-perfect chocolate-box place. The sort of thing you saw in TV series set in the fifties and sixties, with a tiny waiting room and ticket office. There was only one entrance and exit. It was practically deserted except for the staff looking after the ticket office.

Standing next to the metal fencing of the exit, I spotted Scott almost immediately. He looked totally out of place in his skinny jeans, a plain t-shirt, and a leather jacket. His contemporary image didn't fit with the homeliness of the scene.

"Hey, babe!" he called, with a wave.

I walked over to him, pulling my suitcase behind me. Even though I would only be there a few days, I was terrible at packing and had thrown all sorts of clothes in for every eventuality. As the sun beat down on me, I already regretted the big overcoat I wore.

"Here, let me take that." Scott reached over and took the suitcase. "Jesus, Rosie, what the hell have you got in here? Bodies? Did you do away with Mark and think you could dispose of him here?" He let out a low laugh.

His comment would have been funny, except it made me remember the reason for me being here in the first place.

Mark... And his second attempt to get with me.

I shuddered, a chill running over me despite the heat.

Scott noticed my change in mood, and turned to me, his hand touching my forearm. "Sorry, are you okay? Crap joke."

"I'm fine. Still a little shaken up." My gaze fell on the black Range Rover Scott loaded my suitcase into. "Hey, cool ride. I didn't know you had one."

He shrugged. "I don't. Hired it to drive down yesterday. Probably shouldn't have driven though, had a pretty crazy couple of days." He avoided looking at me, no doubt remembering the black-haired woman he'd spent much of those days with instead.

I hopped into the passenger seat and wound down the window. "It's nice to be out of London."

"And Manchester." Scott fired up the engine. "Forgive me if the ride's a little jumpy. I don't usually drive and it's taking me a while to get used to manual gears."

As if to demonstrate, the car bunny hopped towards the exit.

"Shit, sorry."

"Don't worry. It's been so long since I've been behind the wheel myself, I can't even remember how to drive." I laughed.

While Scott drove, I stared out of the window, marvelling at the calming views of the countryside. Almost all of my pent-up stress and emotion over the situation with Mark started to slip away.

The journey from the station only took around fifteen minutes. My jaw dropped as Scott pulled into the driveway of an enormous country house, one of only three on a small estate.

"What the...?"

"Belongs to my mum and my aunt. They clubbed together and bought it after my aunt's first divorce. She swore it was a bolthole for them both whenever things got too tough to handle." His tone was even, but I sensed there was more to it.

"Her first divorce?" I raised my eyebrows. "How many has she had?"

"Fuck knows. She's probably as much of a tart as me."

"How is that even possible?" One corner of my mouth curled up.

"Hey! Not fair."

"Tell me, how many women did you sleep with over the weekend? I saw you in the gossip columns again." I kept the question light, despite not wanting to know the truth.

"None." He shot a sideways glance at me as he parked. "Honestly, Rosie. I haven't been with anyone."

Letting the subject lie, I got out of the car and looked up at the house instead.

Scott hauled my suitcase from the boot. "Let's get inside. I don't know about you, but I'm hungry."

The knot in my stomach was doing a great job of keeping the hunger at bay, but I pretended otherwise. "Mmm, yeah, me too."

The inside of the house lived up to the outside. Decorated in fairly neutral tones, it boasted two living rooms downstairs and an impressive staircase. Without showing me around any further, Scott beckoned for me to follow him upstairs.

"This is your room." He opened a door at the end of a corridor, then gestured to a door next to it. "The bathroom's there."

A calm oasis of blues met me as I walked in. A view of the woodland area to the back of the house greeted me from the window. There was a huge king-sized bed, a white-washed dressing table and chest of drawers, plus a built-in wardrobe. It was everything I loved about country living.

"Wow, it's gorgeous!"

"You didn't think someone as rough as me could have something so beautiful?" It sounded like a joke, but I could sense some underlying meaning in Scott's words. "I'll leave you to unpack. If you need me, my room's the one at the opposite end of the house."

Without another word, he disappeared.

I opened the window, watching the sun slowly set in the sky, and inhaled the clean air, so different to London. If I listened closely, birdsong sounded in my ears, punctuated by the occasional seagull or car. Otherwise, it was blissfully quiet.

Turning back to the room, I let out a long, deep breath. Humming to myself, I unpacked my clothes, then took my wash bag and cosmetics into the bathroom. A claw foot tub dominated the room, leaving me with a longing to take a long, warm soak before bed. My eyelids were already becoming heavy at the thought.

I wanted to forget everything which had happened today - up until now.

Suddenly overwhelmed by everything, I sank down onto the edge of the bed and placed my head in my hands. Silent tears fell down my cheeks as I contemplated exactly what I was doing here.

13

SCOTT

While I waited for Rosie to come downstairs, I cracked open a beer, and examined the contents of the now well-stocked fridge. My cooking skills were non-existent. Evening meals usually consisted of something I could shove in the oven or arrived at my door within minutes. Or were liquid.

With a flourish, I slammed the fridge door shut and turned up the music on my phone. Lost in the moment, I danced around the kitchen, eyes closed, singing along to the track, waving my bottle. With no deadlines, no pressures, no gigs, it was freeing. Much as I loved the band and the lifestyle, sometimes I needed to get away and be on my own. Clear my head, reset.

The sound of someone clearing their throat brought me back to the present.

My eyes flew open to see Rosie standing in the doorway, a grin on her face. "You really are a terrible dancer."

"I'm enjoying myself, not auditioning for that celebrity

dance show." I ground to a halt, not sure whether to be offended by her comment. "Since when are you the expert anyway?"

"Challenge accepted."

She entered the kitchen, and started to step around me, hips swaying in time to the music, totally on the beat. Her entire body moved in perfect harmony, the movements almost hypnotic. I couldn't tear my gaze away. Even dressed casually in an outfit which shrouded her figure, she was mesmerising. If she carried on, we wouldn't need to worry about dinner...

"Okay, okay, stop." I placed my hands on her shoulders, trying to ignore the throbbing in my dick. "You win."

"Yes!" She punched the air and twirled away from me.

I laughed. "Do you want a drink?"

Her shoulders sagged. "Ugh, yes please. I would happily have had several on the train, if only to block out the family who sat next to me. I still have the bruises to prove it."

"Beer? Wine? Gin? Vodka?"

"Are you offering me a cocktail?" A smile threatened the corners of her mouth.

"If that's what you want, Rosie Tatton, then that's what you shall have. I have all the ingredients to make you the best cocktail you have ever tasted." I stepped towards the pantry which housed all the hard spirits.

"Wait, no! Wine will be fine. If you have it."

"I went shopping before you arrived. Pretty much bought the entire supermarket. There's definitely wine." I crooked a finger and beckoned her towards me.

From the selection in the fridge, she chose a dry white wine, added ice and topped it off with soda water.

"I should probably take things easy tonight. Were you going to cook?"

I screwed up one eye and scratched the back of my head. "You honestly think I can?"

It was her turn to laugh. "Sorry, such a dumb question. Do you want me to make something?"

"You're my guest, Rosie, I can't ask you to that."

"Don't be ridiculous. It's my way to say thank you for inviting me."

There were many other ways she could do that, none of which involved a hot meal at the end. But I was trying to be a better man and elevate our relationship. "If you're sure?"

"I'm no Gordon Ramsay, but I make a pretty mean stir fry." She turned to the fridge and set about getting out various ingredients. "Have you got any soy sauce?"

"Fucked if I know." At her request, I set about going through the various cupboards, before finally finding a bottle in the last one I looked in.

While she did the prep, I perched on the edge of the counter. Swigging from my beer, I watched her chop and slice. It was probably the most domestic experience of my life, and I was doing it with the one person I wanted in my bed more than anything. Talk about conflicting interests.

Fifteen minutes later, Rosie placed a dish with noodles, chicken and vegetables on the table. I poured her a second glass of wine and got myself another beer. We sat opposite each other and clinked glasses.

"Cheers!"

"Thanks, Rosie. This is amazing."

"You haven't tasted it yet."

Not wanting to keep her waiting, I forked a good amount into my mouth, savouring the taste. For something she'd knocked up in a few minutes, it really did taste good.

"Mmmhuuhmm."

She frowned. "What's that mean?"

"I stand by my previous comments. This is amazing." I nodded to emphasise the point.

Her cheeks pinked, and she stared down at her bowl. "I've never cooked for anyone before."

It really was a night of firsts.

We ate in silence, the music from my phone the only sound in the room, apart from the odd appreciative murmur. When we'd finished, I pushed the bowl away and leaned back in my chair.

"How are you doing?" I asked. We hadn't spoken about the elephant in the room, the reason why she had come here.

She mirrored my movements, taking a gulp of her wine, then placing the glass back on the table. "I think I'm okay." She chewed on the edge of her thumbnail. "It was a shock to see him there. And when he went on to threaten me again." Her arms wrapped around her body. I wished I could be the one to comfort her. "I had to get away."

"Do you think you should talk to the police about him? He's tried something twice now." I reached for my own glass and sucked in a mouthful of wine. "I don't know what the correct protocol is. After all, you don't necessarily have any concrete proof. I was the one who saw him spike your drink, so it's my word against his. Were there any witnesses at the magazine thing?"

Her shoulders slumped. "I don't know. I guess I don't have anything but anecdotal evidence."

Seeing her defeated had me wanting to gather her in my arms and tell her everything was going to be okay. But I couldn't promise it would be.

"I can tell my management, the model bookers I work with, the people in the industry. Warn them off using him, you know? But then how does that make me look?" Rosie reached for her glass again. "Suddenly, I'm high maintenance and difficult to work with. You have no idea what the industry can be like."

"So he gets away with it because you'll be seen as the troublemaker? That's not fair." My brows knotted together. "Surely after the Me Too movement that's changed?"

Rosie shook her head. "I wish it had. I mean, I've never been subjected to any of the casting couch experiences, thankfully."

"You have friends who have?"

"A few, yeah. Although it was for TV and film parts, not model shoots. But it shouldn't happen."

Her eyes darkened and I wondered whether she was telling the truth. If someone had tried something, I would kill them. My hands balled into fists beneath the table. Seriously, I should have punched that Mark guy out when I had the chance.

"Thank you for this." Rosie gestured around the kitchen with her glass. "It really is good to be away from London for a while. I needed to get away. How long are you staying for?"

"Only until the end of the week. I promised the guys we'd go back in the studio and record some new material." I took a long pull of my beer. "Which gives me precisely four days to come up with a bunch of songs."

"Tell me how it works? Do you come up with the words and someone else does the music? Or do you do it all?"

I wished I could tell her it was all me. That every Trash Gun song was the fruits of my creative endeavours. But I couldn't lie to Rosie. She brought out the goodness in me.

"It depends. Sometimes I'll write something with a definite tune in mind, then Declan and Mat will weave their magic on it. Other times, it's just a collection of words, which they'll work on to make sense of the ideas."

"What inspires you?"

You do, Rosie Tatton, you inspire me.

The words almost slipped from my lips, but I kept them back.

"People, places, moods, feelings."

"Ah, so you do have feelings then." A smile threatened her lips.

"You have no idea."

I hadn't realised I'd spoken the words aloud until I saw Rosie's lips part and she gave a small gasp.

Shit.

Hastily, I backtracked. "I mean, when we've had a brilliant gig, the adrenaline is buzzing, you don't want to come down off that legal high, the sensations, seeing how you're making others react. Sometimes it can be overwhelming. I'll never get tired of it. Ever." I twirled my almost empty beer bottle around in my hand.

"There are times during a gig when you seem to zone out, and get lost in whatever's going on around you," Rosie said, quietly.

It meant something to me that she'd noticed. That she'd taken the time to see *me*, and not just the guy at the front with a mic.

"It still means so much. I know how lucky I am to do a job I absolutely fucking love. I'd hate to get up every morning loathing what I have to do." It was the undeniable truth. Every morning I woke up, grateful as fuck not to have to go to a bank or a shop or whatever. To know I could be creative and lose myself in a world which wasn't always real.

I hadn't opened up to anyone like this before. What had started out with me trying to make sure Rosie was okay had ended up in an almost full confessional.

Yeah, I really did have feelings.

14

ROSIE

S unlight streamed through the curtains, and I blinked at the brightness, taking a couple of moments to realise where I was. Again, apart from the birdsong, everything was quiet. It was an absolute delight.

Scott and I had ended up talking until the small hours. He shared tour stories, no doubt censoring them for my apparently delicate sensibilities, and I told him about the more glamorous shoots I'd done abroad. Throughout the whole night, he didn't make one move on me, except to kiss my cheek when we'd called time on our evening.

The devilish part of me was disappointed he hadn't. The sensible side of my brain told me he was respecting what I'd gone through with Mark. To pounce on me wasn't something a good friend would do.

And that's exactly what Scott was being.

A good friend.

I wasn't used to it.

Confusing didn't even begin to cover it.

A whole day of doing nothing stretched out in front of me.

I couldn't hear any sound in the house. Was Scott still in bed? It was shortly after ten, so I suspected as much. It had been a long time since I'd slept in so late. After a fitful start to the night, tossing and turning, I'd slipped into a deep slumber filled with random dreams of Mark and Scott. Reluctantly, I threw off the cosy duvet and grabbed a sweatshirt to pull on over the vest and shorts combo I'd worn for bed.

Padding barefoot down the stairs, I heard something coming from the cellar. Scott hadn't shown me around the previous evening, but it seemed as if there was someone down there. Quietly, I descended the next flight, only to find him down there strumming on an acoustic guitar, singing to himself.

The final step creaked, and his head jerked up to see me.

"Jesus, are you trying to give me a heart attack?" He clutched a hand to his chest in mock horror.

Noticing he was still dressed in the same clothes as he had been last night, I asked. "Did you even go to bed?"

He blinked and glanced around. "What time is it?"

"Around ten fifteen."

"Shit. No."

My gaze fell on the low coffee table in front of the sofa, where there appeared to be at least half a dozen mugs, all with coffee dregs in them. No wonder he was still awake.

"What were you doing down here anyway?"

He looked at me, then at the guitar, then back to me again. "What do you think?"

"I didn't hear you playing." Then again, it was quite a long way from my room down to here. I suppose, an acoustic guitar didn't really play that loud either.

"Did I disturb you?" His concern appeared genuine.

I shook my head. "I was thinking of getting some breakfast. Do you want anything?"

Scott put down the guitar and stretched. "I should probably get some sleep first."

His answer disappointed me. As he'd invited me to stay, I naively thought we'd spend some time together, go out, at least do something. Watching him sleep hadn't been top of my list of activities.

"Fine. I'll go and raid the fridge." I spun around and stalked up the stairs.

"Wait," he called after me. "If you're cooking, a bacon and egg sandwich would be nice..." I sensed the puppy dog eyes he'd be giving me if I could see his face.

I glanced back at him over my shoulder, seeing the exact expression I'd imagined. "Sure, I guess I should earn my keep somehow."

His gaze raked over my body, lingering at the spot where the end of the sweatshirt met my thighs. He bit his lip, not saying a word. A light shiver shot down my spine, and I had to walk away.

I resumed my place in the kitchen and rustled up some food, calling down to Scott when it was ready. We enjoyed a leisurely breakfast. Scott told me a little more about the house and the village. It sounded much like the trains station had promised: quaint and old-fashioned.

I hoped I would get the opportunity to explore it.

Once we'd finished, Scott leaned back in his chair and yawned widely. "Time to sleep. Will you be okay on your own?"

I shrugged. "I guess so. I'll probably watch some telly or maybe go for a walk."

He stood up and went to leave the room, but not before putting a hand on my shoulder as he passed. "Be careful out there. The village isn't ready for a top model to put in an appearance." Absentmindedly, he kissed the top of my head, his lips leaving an invisible burn mark. "Talking of which, let's go out for dinner tonight. The Kings Arms…"

"Does a mean pie?" I finished, trying to keep from smiling.

He wrinkled his brow. "How do you know that?"

"Insider information." I tapped the side of my nose, thankful for the train guard's suggestion. "Sweet dreams."

"Oh, Rosie, with you in the house, I imagine they will be anything but." And then he was gone.

It had been such a long time since I'd had the time to potter around, take things easy and generally chill out. After I'd cleaned up in the kitchen from this morning's and last night's meals, I headed up to my room.

Gathering up the clothes I planned to wear, I headed into the bathroom. What better way to start the day than with a long, leisurely bath? Sometime later, perfectly relaxed and dressed in a simple pair of jeans and an oversized jumper, I grabbed my phone and went downstairs to the living room. I settled down on the sofa, stretching my legs out in front of me. As I was about to turn on the television, my phone pinged.

Saff: Where are you? I haven't heard from you in a couple of days…are you on a shoot? xx

Saff had no knowledge of what had gone on with Mark. I hadn't chosen to share the details with my best friend, instead I'd gone to my friend with benefits. She at least deserved to know some of the details.

I called her back instead of messaging. She picked up on the second ring.

"Sorry, I didn't mean to sound needy, but we haven't been in touch since dinner after Brixton. Something seemed off. Is everything okay?"

The sunlight poured through the window, casting light and heat across my body. Right now, everything seemed fine.

"Yeah, all's good. I, um, decided to come away for a few days." It wasn't a total lie. "A couple of castings recently have taken it out of me." *How pathetic did I sound?*

"Poor you. Must be awful prancing around in expensive clothes having someone do your hair and make-up for you." Saff wasn't having any of it. "Meanwhile, I'm trying to stop Tris tearing down a wall, just because he thinks it will make the kitchen/diner more open plan."

I laughed. Saff Barnes was the least domesticated person I knew. Hearing her talk about DIY tasks was alien. I ached to feel the same way about someone.

"Anyway, where are you? Are you with friends?"

How to answer? What would she think if I told her I was at Scott's place?

"Mmmhmm, it's one of the girls from the agency. You wouldn't know her. She's got a place in the country," I bluffed.

"Ooo, fancy! I guess I'll see pics on your socials?"

"Maybe. She's a bit funny about people posting stuff." God, I really was getting good at lying to my best friend. I didn't know how Saff would react if she knew I was with Scott.

"But you're okay though?" Saff's tone softened. It was good to know she actually did care about what was going on with me.

"Yes, absolutely fine. Enjoying some rest and relaxation." It was well after midday and I hadn't checked a single email or posted anything to my social media. So refreshing. I had something to thank Scott for after all.

"Okay, well, good. You should have spoken to me sooner though. I thought there was something wrong when we were at dinner the other night."

I winced, remembering the hangover which had followed. Drinking to erase the memory of Scott running out on me again was nothing new though.

"You're right, I should have. I'm sorry, Saff."

"Don't be! As long as you're sure everything's okay?"

"It is."

"Then have a fabulous time with your ridiculously beautiful friend, and don't forget about me."

"Ha, as if! I'll be back soon."

We said our goodbyes and hung up. I stopped myself

from checking my emails, they could wait. It wasn't as if I was likely to get the *Aspire* job after yesterday, and I'd already cried off my appointments for the rest of this week.

Finding the remote, I switched on the telly and channel hopped until I found something worth watching. *Step Up* for the eleventy billionth time would work perfectly. And I watched all of about half an hour of it before falling asleep.

15

SCOTT

S he looked absolutely gorgeous sleeping. The light honey colour of her skin, exposed by the shoulder of her jumper slipping down, looked good enough to eat. Her hair draped around like a blonde cloud. And she made the cutest little muttering noises.

It would be a shame to wake her.

I hovered by the sofa, torn between wanting to shake her awake and leaving her be.

The TV remote had fallen on the floor, and I bent down to pick it up, only to drop it again. It clattered against the leg of the coffee table with a bang.

Rosie's eyelids fluttered open, the amber colour of her irises even more vibrant than usual. "How long have I been asleep?" she yawned.

"We're on *Step Up 3D* if that helps quantify it?" I grinned at her choice of movie.

"Humph, the last thing I remember is Channing Tatum..." Her eyes glassed over.

I'd never seen the film, but I knew who Channing Tatum was. Lucky bastard. I lifted up her feet, sat down on the sofa and lowered them into my lap. "Are you still up for going out?"

Rosie shifted herself into a sitting position, easing her legs back underneath her. "Sure. I guess I don't have to get too dressed up?"

"Babe, it's a village pub. You could go as you are. No-one would bat an eyelid."

"I'm sure they wouldn't, but I have to get changed. I can't go out in the same clothes I've worn during the day." She nibbled on her thumbnail. "It doesn't seem right."

"Go on, live a little. You look great."

She pulled the sweater up to cover her shoulder. "I probably look a mess after being asleep."

"Trust me, you could never look a mess." I reached over and tucked a strand of her blonde hair behind her ear, my thumb grazing her jawline as I pulled away.

Her breath hitched, and my hand stilled. It would be oh-so-easy to lean over and kiss her, taste those plump, rose pink lips. I swallowed as the air between us charged.

"I guess I'll go and get ready," she said, breaking the moment.

After she'd left the room, I let my head slump back on the edge of the sofa and stared at the ceiling. *Shit, why did she turn me into a teenage boy with a crush?*

The Kings Arms was quiet on a Tuesday evening. I hadn't bothered calling ahead and booking a table. The staff there knew my family well, and usually accommodated us even when it was busy. The waitress showed us to a table in an alcove towards the back of the pub, nicely secluded and away from the rest of the customers.

Despite me telling Rosie she didn't have to make too much effort, she'd changed into a floral-patterned dress, which stopped mid-thigh, and a pair of low-heeled black boots. The mix of vintage and biker vibes really suited her. She'd pulled her thick blonde hair into a messy bun, strands framing her face. My fingers itched to run through it and pull the locks down around her shoulders. I practically had to sit on my hands to stop myself.

"Can I get you two some drinks?" The waitress looked between us, no doubt ready to tell her friends that Scott Lincoln and Rosie Tatton were in her pub.

"I'll have a beer," I replied, and glanced over at Rosie who was engrossed in the wine list. "Did you want to get a bottle?"

"Scott Lincoln, are you trying to get me drunk?" Rosie asked in mock horror.

"What do you think, babe?" I waggled my eyebrows at her.

The waitress appeared to be holding her breath as she waited patiently for us to make a decision.

"Can we have the Argentinian Malbec please?" Rosie placed the laminated wine list on the table, and then leaned back in her chair. "You'll share some with me, won't you?"

"Of course. I couldn't let you drink alone."

"Good choice." She scribbled down the drinks, then looked up again, pen poised over her pad. "And are you ready to order food?"

"I need a few more minutes," said Rosie. "If you can get

our drinks, I promise to be ready by the time you come back."

The waitress nodded and walked off, leaving us alone.

Having been there several times before, I knew the menu pretty much by heart and always ordered the same chicken, leek and bacon pie. Whether the menu was Rosie's cup of tea, I had no idea. As a model, I guessed she had to watch what she ate, maybe a carb heavy selection of food wasn't the best suggestion. Still, there wasn't anywhere else in the vicinity where we could eat out easily.

"There are so many things I could have..." sighed Rosie. "Too much to choose from."

"You'll have to be quick." I gestured to the waitress walking over with our drinks.

"Argh." Rosie shook her head, her fingers circling the laminated menu before finally settling on something. "Okay. I hope I don't regret it."

"Here you go." The waitress put the bottle of wine, two glasses and my beer on the table. She stepped back, pen poised over the pad, looking expectantly at Rosie.

"Could I have the chicken, leek and bacon pie, please?" she said.

A grin spread across my face. We were clearly compatible.

Sitting at a table opposite a woman who had such an affect on me was a strange sensation.

In all the time we'd known each other, we'd rarely done something as mundane as go out for a meal. Most times it had been stolen moments backstage or in a club, followed by smouldering hot sex; fast, slow, dirty... breathtakingly dirty. Hotel rooms had been our go to place, nameless, face-less, inconsequential.

Now, I was facing those consequences by inviting her to a place which was so close to my heart, personal to my family, my haven.

Surely she had to realise what that meant?

"Mmm, this is delicious." Rosie licked her lips in appre-ciation. "Can I try some of the mash?"

She'd ordered her meal without carbs, but the way she hungrily eyed my potato amused me.

"Sure you're ready for such decadence?" I teased, forking up a small amount for her. I lifted it to her lips, watching it disappear into her mouth. Small moans of enjoyment emanated from her. How I'd love to hear those same murmurings coming from her when I buried my head between her legs.

"Heavenly!" she breathed and closed her eyes.

My dick twitched as she threw her head back in mock passion. I wanted to replicate that expression for her when we got back to the house later. My appetite for food all but disappeared and I put the knife and fork together on my plate. "You want to get out of here?"

She finished her mouthful before speaking. "Now? Aren't we going to get dessert?"

The thought of licking ice cream off her perfectly toned stomach reignited my cravings, I got harder as a result. "There's dessert back at the house. And I won't have to restrain myself from doing bad things to you in a public place." I reached across the table and gently stroked the back of her hand. "That's if you want to, of course."

Rosie moved her thumb over my knuckles. "Why wouldn't I want to?"

Her touch inflamed my entire body, adrenalin fizzled around my bloodstream.

"Then let's go."

16

ROSIE

Holding hands with Scott Lincoln was a first.

After we decided to leave the pub, we practically ran back to the house, him gripping my hand tight.

We crashed through the front door, and Scott pulled me into the living room.

I discarded my jacket, then kicked off my boots, while Scott did the same, his eyes never leaving mine. He closed the distance between us, strong arms wrapping around me, pulling me flush to his body. His fingers tugged at the hem of my dress, lifting it upwards and over my head. Cool air hit the backs of my thighs. I stood in front of him in only a peony pink bra and knicker set. Instinctively, I parted my legs; I wanted him to touch me.

"Patience," he whispered into my neck, his lips brushing a line along my collarbone and up to my ear.

My skin prickled, goose bumps forming where his lips had been.

Scott had never been good with patience. Usually we were naked by now, knowing which buttons to press to get the other off. Hot, sweaty, driven sex designed with one outcome in mind.

This was different.

Slow, sensual, exquisite torture.

He slid down to his knees, his face directly level with my groin. Looking up to gauge my expression, he hooked his thumbs into my knickers and drew them down my legs.

I gasped, feeling his breath against me.

"Pretty," he rasped, tossing the lacy garment to one side. "Although unnecessary right now…"

Taking his time, he gently stroked my right inner thigh, fingertips calloused from playing guitar enhancing the gentle sensations. I bit my lip, wanting him to go faster, needing him to. Desperate to rub my thighs together to get some kind of pressure where I needed it most, I wriggled around trying to dictate where Scott would touch me next.

Turns out I wasn't great at patience either. A less than delicate slap on my left arse cheek had me up on my toes.

I puffed out a breath. "Owww."

"A little self-restraint, Rosie, please. Unless you want to be tied down while I make you come with my tongue." Scott's tone rumbled low, cautionary, thick with lust.

Heat flooded through me at the thought. My eyes closed and I let my head fall back, placing my hands on Scott's shoulders to steady myself; helpless to do anything other than be overwhelmed by all the sensations he could create.

He continued on his slow journey around my inner thighs, grazing my clit as he did so. I tensed, wishing he'd linger or at least move his mouth there like he'd promised. I was molten lava in his hands, everything focused on him and his movements.

Gently, he slipped one finger inside me, followed by another, his thumb finally landing where I'd been craving it most. A satisfied sigh escaped my lips. The delicate motion had me contracting around his hand, nothing rushed, no haste, every movement designed to give me the ultimate pleasure. He continued to torment me, bringing me so close to the edge, then pulling back. Each one of my senses worked overtime and I tried to stop toppling into the abyss. My knees began to shake as the first flush of a release built up inside my belly. Scott sensed the change and increased the pressure of his thumb, the nails of his other hand digging into my buttock. My breath came in rapid gasps as I fought against the sensations racking my body, until everything unravelled, white lights exploding.

Scott looked up at me, one corner of his mouth curled at the edge. He licked his lips. "That work for you, babe?"

I slapped his shoulder. "You really have to ask?"

He got to his feet. "Ready for round two?"

"There's more?"

"You got yours, now it's my turn." Without warning, he scooped me up in his arms and tossed me on the sofa as if I weighed nothing at all.

While I watched him peel off his t-shirt, I unhooked my bra and added it to the pile of clothes on the floor. I loved his slightly wiry body, with the smattering of tattoos marking his skin. He wasn't muscular like a lot of the male models I worked with, but the energy he expended on stage went some way to keeping him in shape. He unbuttoned his jeans, and his rock-hard erection pushed against his boxers. My breath caught. With one hand, he found his wallet and pulled a condom out, while the other pushed down his jeans and boxers. Naked, he rolled the condom over his dick, then moved towards me. He placed a knee either side of my hips and slid his body down lower. His mouth crashed against mine first, tongue exploring the seam of my lips, then pressing inside. I gripped his shoulders again, lifting my leg to wrap around his waist as he positioned himself to drive into me. The easy familiarity of him moving inside me had me pulling him deeper with each thrust. I wasn't sure I could take any more as we rocked together in total synchronisation, the ease of our closeness telling. Scott's release came unusually quickly, and he collapsed beside me, wrapping his arms around my body.

"I'm sorry," he breathed.

"What for?" I couldn't see his face, unsure of what he meant.

"I wanted it to be more..." When he didn't say anything else, I shifted my position so I could look into his eyes.

"More?" I encouraged.

A dark shadow fell over his features. "Different. This isn't a hotel room. You're here. I..." He fell silent again.

"And?"

He chewed on his lip before answering. "I don't bring women here. You're the first one."

This was a revelation. Given this was a country hideaway, I'd have thought it was the ideal place for him to bring his various flings. Clearly it wasn't.

I felt honoured.

"I want to sleep with you," Scott whispered in my ear.

"Didn't we just do that?"

He took my chin and turned my face to his. "No, I mean sleep with you. Wake up with you."

It was possibly the most intimate thing he'd ever said to me. I couldn't remember ever staying the night with him, even when we'd dated.

Mutely, I nodded. We got to our feet. Scott took my hand and led me upstairs to his bedroom.

The bed was perfectly made, which surprised me. I had him pegged as a mussed up, messy bed kind of guy. Then again, I'd gotten a few things wrong about him recently.

Without a word, he lifted the covers and indicated for me to slide underneath the crisp cotton. I shivered as the cool material hit my overheated skin. Scott slid in and spooned me. The unexpected feel of his skin so close to mine made me shudder all over again.

He nuzzled the back of my neck. "Goodnight, Rosie. Sleep well."

"You too." I snuggled into his embrace and closed my eyes.

Within minutes, I'd fallen into a deep sleep, my dreams full of Scott.

17

SCOTT

ho else has a breakfast of fruit and pancakes at..." Rosie glanced up at the huge railway clock on the wall. "Two o'clock in the afternoon?"

We had resumed our position on the couch in the living room, albeit semi-dressed, after a lazy morning lying in bed, talking, touching, exploring. Neither of us had bothered to shower yet, hunger for food rather than each other, taking precedence.

I'd made an effort: microwaved a bunch of readymade pancakes and chucked a load of pre-prepared fruit into a bowl. Topped it with some thick Greek yoghurt and maple syrup, and voila: breakfast of champions. I'd even made a cafetière of coffee. My culinary skills were improving.

Rosie crossed her legs and tucked the throw around them. She reached for another piece of melon, sucking the juice off her fingers, making my cock twitch. She looked utterly, gloriously, fuckable, dressed only in an old Trash

Gun t-shirt she'd found in my room, her hair mussed up and tumbling over her shoulders.

"Why have we never done this before?" she mused; a question I'd already thought of. Having spent yesterday together and then waking up in the same bed without of one of us—okay, me—running out. It was different. Actually talking, and genuinely enjoying each other's company, came as a total revelation. I'd always suspected Rosie and I had a true connection, but I'd always been too stubborn to see it.

"What? Have fucking amazing sex? We've always done that." I winked, trying to deflect the real feelings I wrestled with.

She threw a raspberry at me. I made a big deal of catching it, then putting it between my teeth and sucking on it. My gaze fell to her chest, giving her every indication of where my mind was.

"You know what I mean." She gestured to the breakfast trays, and us curled up on the sofa. "This."

I softened. "Makes a change, doesn't it?"

"But why now?"

Oh, she was full of questions this morning. Perhaps that was one of the reasons I never stayed the night. I didn't know how to answer her. I didn't know why now. I didn't really know what had changed to make me think differently. Seeing her so vulnerable after Mark tried to spike her hit me hard. I'd wanted to look after her, protect her, make sure she came to no harm. All things I hadn't never felt before. Maturity, was that it? Stepping up and taking responsibility for someone. I gulped down some coffee to quell the butter-flies in my stomach.

No.

Not maturity.

Love.

I fucking loved her.

Her beautiful blue eyes were fixed on me, blinking as she waited for my answer.

I choked.

I couldn't tell her. Even though every fibre of my being screamed at me to stop being a naive idiot, the words wouldn't come. If I put myself out there and she didn't feel the same, I didn't know what I'd do. Die of shame, probably.

No. I had to be the Scott Lincoln she knew. The one who didn't give a fuck, who seemingly didn't care, the one who was only into her for the benefits.

I hated myself, but I couldn't do it. I simply couldn't do it.

Putting my mug down on the table, I picked up a strawberry and dipped it in the yoghurt and syrup mix. Holding it close to her lips, I teased her with it.

"Do you want it? It's so juicy and delicious..."

Rosie laughed and leaned forward to take it in her mouth. "So, so tempting."

"I could say the same about you." I drew back, holding it just out of reach. "How much do you want it?"

"Are you talking about the strawberry or...?" Her mouth curved into a mischievous smile.

Without saying another word, I pounced on her, flipping her onto her back and stripping the t-shirt from her body in one swift move. Lazily, I traced the creamy tip of the fruit down her sternum, leaving a smear of red juice and syrup as I did.

"Scott," she breathed. I repeated the trail with my tongue, licking the sticky trail from her skin. "I think this couch has seen enough action, don't you?"

Reluctantly, I broke away, knees pressed either side of her hips, and stared down at her. "Does that mean you need cleaning up?"

"Well..."

I didn't give her chance to say another word as I scooped her up into my arms and carried her upstairs. When I got to my room, I kicked open the door and headed into the en-suite. Dropping Rosie onto her feet, I reached into the shower and turned on the waterfall shower head to full power. I stripped off my boxers and t-shirt, before extending a hand to Rosie and dragging her beneath the jets.

"Shit! It's cold!" she squealed.

"Sorry." I reached past her and knocked the temperature up a notch or two. "You don't know how many cold showers I've had to have because of you."

She shivered and pulled me towards her.

"Let me get rid of that sticky mess between your breasts." I cocked an eyebrow. "Unless you want more?"

Her gaze fell on my dick, already at half-mast. Seriously, just being around the woman got me aroused. Rosie placed her hands on my hips and slithered down to her knees, her head in the direct line of my crotch. I braced myself against the shower wall as her mouth closed around the tip of my cock. She wrapped one hand around my base, her hot tongue dragging up and down my shaft, water cascading over her head and body. One of my hands cupped the back of her head, fingers tightening in her hair, and I closed my eyes, trying to breathe. My head fell backwards as took the length of me, and I felt my cock flex in her mouth. *So, so close...*

Rosie swallowed and gave a little cough, sucking in her bottom lip, as she stared up at me.

I pulled her to her feet, my mouth on hers, able to taste me on her lips. The water crashing around us dipped a couple of degrees and I reached over to turn it up again. Without saying another word, I drew back and reached for the shower gel. Lathering some up on my hands, the lemony scent became overpowering. Slowly, I ran my palms over her skin, soaping her up and washing away the strawberry and yoghurt residue. Her nipples pebbled from the attention I bestowed on them, my gaze never leaving hers. I continued my path down her body, the water washing away the soap until there was none left. When I reached between Rosie's legs, her knees buckled. She steadied herself against me, and I gently stroked her, watching closely as her pupils became so large, they almost eclipsed the blue iris. I increased the pressure, inserted one digit, then a second, seeing her gasp and clutch at my shoulder. A strangled breath escaped her. She contracted around my fingers, her body convulsing in pleasure.

A crooked grin crept across my face once I'd withdrawn my fingers. "Ready for a shower now?"

Rosie beat her fists against my chest, laughter spilling from her lips. "You're incorrigible, Scott Lincoln."

I saluted her. "Babe, I try my best."

18

ROSIE

I t was only the second time we'd ever woken up together. After our shower the previous afternoon, we'd lay on Scott's bed, watching movies and talking about music and the band, my modelling shoots, and a million other things besides. It almost felt as if we were a real couple.

One of Scott's arms wrapped around me, the other hand rested between my legs. Gently, I stretched, trying to get some friction between our skin.

Last night had meant more to me than any of the other nights we'd spent together.

Actually talking and discovering what made him tick. Not just experiencing the unbridled lust we usually shared but making that deeper connection which real couples had. When he'd peered into my eyes during my last orgasm, my entire being melted. The intensity of his stare, the raw emotion of his release, my skin rippled all over again.

How did we move on from this?

Breakfast in bed might be a good start.

Trying not to wake him, I slid out from beneath him.

I grabbed his t-shirt and pulled it over my head as I marvelled at the sight of his naked body tangled in the sheets, seeing him properly for the first time.

The smile spreading across my face was totally genuine as I padded downstairs after taking a pit stop in the bathroom. Just before I reached the kitchen, I heard the sound of the coffee machine. Was there any way Scott could have got downstairs before me? No, it was impossible. Someone else was in the house. My eyes darted from side to side, seeking a weapon to protect me. If I thought about it rationally, a burglar wouldn't exactly make themselves coffee before they helped themselves to the contents of the house.

Nervously, I poked my head into the room.

Standing at the sink, humming quietly to herself, was an impossibly glamorous grey-haired woman. Dressed in what looked like a Pucci print dress which finished mid-calf, her hair was fastened in a chic chignon. She certainly didn't look like a burglar.

"Um, hello?" I called.

The woman clutched a hand to her chest and turned to face me. "Goodness, my dear, you scared me."

"And you me." My brows knotted together, and I studied her more closely; a vague hint of recognition creeping in. "What are you doing here?"

Her gaze swept up and down me, and I regretted not putting on more clothes. While Scott's t-shirt skimmed the tops of my thighs, I was buck naked underneath. Any excessive movement, and I'd be flashing her more than I should within minutes of meeting the woman.

"Vivan Woods. Scott's aunt." She appraised me once more. "And I know who you are, Rosie. You came to one of my charity dinners recently."

I clicked my fingers. "Yes! That's right, the one for domestic abuse survivors. How much did you raise in the end?"

"That, my dear, is neither here nor there." She turned back to the sink. "I'm guessing you must be here with my nephew, considering my son arrived with me, and was alone."

There was another man in the house? I tried to tug the t-shirt down to make myself more presentable. "Your son?"

"Yes, Sebastian. I'm sure you'll meet him later. Now what were you doing down here in the first place?"

"Breakfast. I was going to make breakfast for me and Scott and take it back to bed," I managed, quite unused to interacting with someone like Vivian.

"Then don't let me stop you." She finished making the coffee which had alerted me to her presence, brandishing the espresso cup in my direction. "I'm almost done here, then I'll be going out into the garden."

"Rosie! Where are you? I'm not done with you yet!" Scott's voice floated into the room nanoseconds before his arrival.

Both Vivian and I turned to see him leap into the room, totally naked, sporting an impressive lazy erection.

The three of us screamed at the same time. Scott

grabbed the closest thing to him - a copy of the Guardian - to cover his modesty.

"Shit, Vivian what the hell are you doing here?"

She rolled her eyes at him. "It is my house, Scott. I can come here whenever I wish." Taking a tiny sip of coffee, she spoke. "More to the point, what are you doing here?"

"I told Bas I was coming down, I thought he would mention it to you."

"You know Sebastian, he's not always great at the detail."

Between them, they were painting quite the picture of the elusive Sebastian, Scott's cousin. I was intrigued to meet him.

"Is he here?" asked Scott, rustling the newspaper around his hips.

"Somewhere. I'm sure you'll catch up with him at some point." Emptying the dregs of her coffee into the sink, Vivian rinsed her cup and placed it on the draining board. "I'll leave you two alone. Rosie, lovely to see you again. We'll have afternoon tea and catch up some more." With a wink, she headed out into the garden.

I let out a hard breath, before the giggles started. "How embarrassing was that?"

Scott tossed the newspaper onto the table and closed the distance between us, pressing his dick against me. "Not as bad for you as it was for me." He slid a hand underneath his t-shirt, his thumb caressing my clit. "Although..."

"Stop, we can't...your cousin is around here somewhere. I don't want him walking in on us." I wriggled against his thumb, wishing we were alone.

"Spoilsport." He kissed the end of my nose and pulled away. "Now did you say something about breakfast?"

"Only if you get dressed, disappointing though that thought is." I grinned. "And can you bring me a pair of knickers?"

"Do I have to?" he pouted.

"I am not flashing your aunt again! And God only knows when your cousin will appear."

"Good point. I don't want Bas anywhere near you."

His throwaway comment made my insides contract. I didn't want any other man near me either.

While he went to get some clothes, I cobbled together a breakfast of avocado, eggs, salmon and toast with lashings of coffee. The caffeine would at least help me to stay awake.

"I didn't realise Vivian and Bas would be coming," Scott said, shoving a fork heaped with eggs into his mouth.

"She obviously didn't realise you'd be here either."

"We don't exactly have a family booking system in operation. Usually it's a quick message to the group to see what people's plans are."

"And I guess you didn't fill them in on yours?"

He chewed on the crust of his slice of toast, wrinkling his nose. "Can't remember. Might have mentioned something about me being here."

"But not that you'd have a guest?" I pressed, wondering if he'd had this planned all along and his invite hadn't come out of nowhere.

He threw his head back, eyes fixed on the ceiling in frustration. "Doubt it. I don't make a habit of bringing anyone here."

Despite his tone, the words at least made me feel special. If I was the first person he'd brought here, it had to mean something. Didn't it?

Scott pushed his plate away, then stood up. "I'm going to get a shower."

"Shall I join you?" I lowered my gaze and looked up at him through hooded eyes.

"Not with Viv and Bas around. Another time."

He shut me down. Contrary fucker.

After he'd left the room, I cleared the table, put the plates in the dishwasher, and poured myself another coffee. I stood at the sink, looking out over the back garden. Vivian tended to some bushes with flowers on. There was no point in my trying to identify them, my green fingers were black.

"She likes gardening. Especially here. Her London place only has a balcony." A male voice said from behind me.

I turned, seeing a tall, dark haired man, dressed in jeans and a t-shirt. He had similar sharp features to Vivian, albeit darker, and a gym-honed body. I assumed this was Scott's cousin.

"Sebastian?"

The corner of his mouth curled up and he approached me, holding out his hand. "Bas, please."

His handshake was firm, his fingers curling around mine.

"Rosie."

"Oh, I know who you are. Such a shame my cousin got his sticky paws on you before I had the chance to meet you properly." He released me and stepped back, appraising me.

Suddenly self-conscious, I was still only wearing Scott's

t-shirt and a tiny pair of knickers, I backed away, my arse bumping into the edge of the cupboard. "Are you staying here for long?" I asked, desperate to change the subject and bring it back to safer ground.

"Couple of days, probably. Mum said Scott was going to be here. I haven't seen him for a while, so thought it would be good to catch up. Didn't know he'd already have company though." Bas winked at me.

A hot flush crept over my whole body. If circumstances had been different, I'd have played up to Bas's flirting. But I wanted to find out could be anything more between Scott and me. Last night, he'd alluded to it, but his behaviour this morning indicated otherwise.

Now that we had guests, I guess I might find out.

19

SCOTT

"Punching, mate, absolutely punching." Bas pushed his way into my room and slumped down on the bed. "How the hell did you pull her?"

Sebastian Rafferty: almost as much of a man whore as me, which was saying something. Although just year younger, he was at least as much trouble. Not to mention competition. Despite me being the more famous relative, he usually ended up with the girl if we happened to be interested in the same one. As far as I could tell, when he wasn't dabbling in the modelling world, he ponced about in clubs pretending to be a promoter or something and sponged off his mother. With his razor-sharp cheekbones and blond hair, he never appeared to be short of jobs when he needed them. The product of Vivian's third, and happiest, marriage, he was her only child. And boy, didn't he act like it.

"None of your business."

"You two are exclusive though? Serious? I wouldn't want to waste my time." He gave me a wink.

Suddenly, I was the grown up, not a feeling I was used to around Bas. "We're..." I ground to a halt. I honestly didn't know what we were. Last night was everything I'd wanted, and then some. But we hadn't had the opportunity to discuss what the next step was. Logically, it pointed to something more serious, but I didn't know if Rosie wanted the same.

"Mum's probably already talking to her about engagement parties and weddings."

Vivian had taken Rosie into the village for afternoon tea. I suspected it would involve more gin than tea, but who was I to say otherwise? The two of them spending time together alone made me nervous. I'd never introduced any of my girlfriends to my family before. For all I knew, by the time Vivian had finished regaling Rosie with tales from my childhood, she may not want anything to do with me.

"I'd appreciate it if you didn't try and make a move on her." I stared at my reflection in the mirror as I said the words, meaning every single one of them. I didn't want Bas - or anyone else - touching her, thinking about her, lusting after her. I wanted all of those things for myself.

"Shame." Bas slapped a hand against his thigh. "Don't suppose you want to go into town tonight then? Get into a club?"

I couldn't think of anything I'd like less. The past couple of days, chilling out here, had calmed my restless streak. The thought of being around crowds of other people, brought me out in hives.

"Not tonight, mate."

"Got a hot date with blondie?" He waggled his eyebrows. "Taking her down the pub again?"

I tossed a wet towel at his head. "Fuck off."

Honestly, I didn't know what we would do. My head buzzed with inspiration again, and I wanted to get more lyrics down. But I also wanted to spend time with Rosie. Quality time, not just exploring every inch of her body, although that would be acceptable too.

Then my aunt and cousin had turned up and skewed the dynamics.

There hadn't been a plan. I hadn't invited Rosie here to end up in a relationship with her. She needed a break from London and all the shit she'd been through. I had simply offered her a retreat. Anything else was a bonus.

Emotions really were turning out to be a total headfuck.

Not knowing if you know...
How I feel...
Is killing me...
Adjust my reality...
Make this real for me...

I sang the words over and over, trying to find the right cadence. It wasn't happening. I was trying too hard. Trying to make it the epic Trash Gun song to stand on a level with *Wasted By My Side*. Initially, I'd tried it as a power ballad, knowing Declan would be able to create an awesome riff for the bridge - Slash style from *November Rain*. It didn't work. Next, I'd amped it up. Tried to make it something everyone could jump around to. Absolutely fucking not. Finally, I grabbed the acoustic again, slowed the whole thing down, and strummed some softer chords.

Instantly, I knew I'd nailed it.

Wasted paled into insignificance beside this. Once I'd decided on a title, it would be perfect.

I grabbed my phone and recorded the chorus, knowing the sound quality of an Apple device wouldn't necessarily do it justice. Then I sent the clip to Declan, Mat and Bobby. No message, no explanation.

Then I waited.

Mat: what the fuck is this, man???

Bobby: where the hell did this come from??

Declan: I can already hear the bridge

Declan never failed to deliver on expectation.

Scott: a little something I rustled up on my break

Mat: amazing what you can do when you're not fucked up on coke

Scott: wanker

Mat: telling the truth though, aren't I?

To some extent he was. There was a pile of other half-finished songs and lyrics which had come from the other night's session, which weren't quite as pure. None of them were as heartfelt as this. The words had poured out of me, almost vomiting over the page. I knew they'd need refining, but the concept was there.

And I knew the inspiration behind them.

She was currently with my aunt.

Scott: maybe. Dec, can you do something with this?

Declan: already thinking about it, gimme a couple of hours, I'll send you a sample

Fuck I loved these guys. This was what made us tick, how we worked. We were all on a similar plane, vibing off each other, even if we weren't in the same room. Excitement at actually recording the song zipped through me. Getting back to Manchester and into the studio couldn't come soon enough.

Scott: looking forward to it already

Bobby: not much call for a drum beat here, is there? #Disappointed

He followed it up with a laughing emoji. I could already picture it being played live as well, and sadly for Bobby there wouldn't need to be much involvement from him. We hadn't really done much acoustic stuff before, preferring to keep the energy on a high. Maybe now was the time for us to mature, to grow up.

Scott: don't worry, mate, I've got plenty of other material you can play around with

Bobby: excellent! Don't keep me hanging

Declan: got something already, gonna hop off and record it...laters!

I itched to hear what he would come up with.

Scott: cool, speak soon

Satisfied with the exchange, I tossed the phone on the sofa. Creative adrenaline at its best, I grabbed the guitar again and messed around with some other chord phrases, knowing Declan would be doing the same.

More lyrics bubbled up, and I couldn't get them down

on paper quick enough. Most of them were utter shit and made no sense, but it was good to get them out. It helped structure my thoughts. When I read them back, they were definitely different to what I'd written before. If I stepped back and looked at them rationally, I'd basically written an album's worth of love songs.

Trash Gun didn't do that.

I didn't do that.

Rosie Tatton really had got under my skin.

Casting aside the guitar once more, I lay back on the sofa, laced my hands behind my head, and stared up at the white ceiling. A myriad of questions swirled around in my brain.

Could we make this work?

How could I get rid of my aunt and cousin to find out?

Did Rosie even want this?

The latter scared me the most. What if I'd got it all wrong and she didn't want anything more than to keep our friends-with-benefits gig going.

She hadn't dated anyone seriously in the past few months, at least not that I'd known about. I'd taken a few women out, nothing to write home about. Also, I hadn't slept with anyone. Sure, I'd acted as if I had, and there were internet gossip stories to seemingly prove it - or disprove it, depending on your opinion.

Without truly realising it, I'd been comparing everyone to Rosie.

And no-one measured up.

How was I going to approach it with her? We'd never really had a proper heart to heart about our relationship.

Hell, neither of us had ever even classed what we had as a relationship.

The closest we'd come had been last night, when we'd fallen asleep together.

I wished Vivian and Bas weren't around, and it was still just Rosie and I here.

But I had to work with the parameters I had.

Perhaps I could persuade them to go out tonight, and I could cook.

I actually laughed out loud, my chuckle reverberating around the room.

I'd never cooked for anyone; I rarely even did for myself.

Giving Rosie food poisoning would be one way of finding out how she felt about me, as I held her hair while she was being sick.

I needed to talk to her before I drove myself bat shit crazy with not knowing.

If she didn't feel the same, I didn't know what I was going to do.

20

ROSIE

I found Vivian Woods absolutely fascinating.

When she'd suggested afternoon tea, I hesitated, almost feeling guilty leaving Scott. As he'd been kind enough to invite me to the house, I sensed I should spend time with him.

Hell, I wanted to spend time with him. After last night, I'd woken up with a confusion of feelings clouding my chest. The sex was, as ever, amazing. For two people who hooked up occasionally, we knew each other well, knowing the movements which gave the other the most pleasure. There had been a different level of intimacy though, not just the usual frenzied lust which came from wanting each other so badly, something more, something deeper. Something which connected on an emotional as well as a physical level. It surprised me. I'd spent so long trying to deny my actual feelings, I didn't know what to feel any more.

I wanted to talk to Scott, try to find out how he saw things.

But right now, I was stuck in a tea shop with his aunt.

Vivian seemed almost a minor celebrity around the village. Every shop assistant greeted her like a long-lost friend. She'd been given freebies, discounts, you name it. A cluster of carrier bags around her feet provided the evidence.

"How long have you and Scott been seeing each other?" Vivian clearly didn't believe in beating around the bush. She sipped her tea from a delicate china cup, her eyes scanning the sandwiches and cakes as she decided what to have.

"Oh, we're not," I muttered, chewing on one of the tiny salmon and cucumber sandwiches. "We're friends."

She raised her eyebrows. "So you walking around his kitchen half naked, until he turns up with morning glory is what you kids are classing as friendship these days?"

I almost choked on my mouthful. I hadn't expected those words to slip from Vivian's prim lips. Coughing, I reached for my water glass and took a sip, trying to stop my eyes from watering. "We, um, have benefits to that friendship."

"As I can see."

It was hard to tell whether she disapproved or not. I didn't know her well enough to know whether she was joking with me. If it were me and my mother, she would definitely have been taking the piss out of the situation, more than likely making some lewd comment about Scott's girth. Vivian Woods didn't possess that kind of gutter humour.

"There's something between the two of you though, isn't there?"

Was there? If even someone who had only seen the two of us together for the briefest of moments could see it, why couldn't we? Or at least, why couldn't we acknowledge it?

I let out a sigh, the macaroons crying out to me. "We enjoy each other's company," I said instead.

"It's more than that, though, Rosie. I can see how he looks at you. You know he's never brought a girl back to the house before." Vivian poured herself another cup of tea. "In all the time we've had it."

More revelations. If she kept going at this rate, I wasn't sure I'd be able to look Scott in the eye by the time we got home.

"He told me. I'm honoured." A small smile crept across my face.

"Did Scott tell you how we bought the house?" Vivian changed the subject.

I nodded. "Yes, you and your sister invested in it."

"It was our escape." Vivian lowered her eyes. "My first marriage wasn't a pleasant one. My ex was violent towards me. I never had anywhere I could class as a bolt hole when I needed to get away. When he finally paid out on a settlement, I promised myself we'd always have somewhere to go. Somewhere safe, peaceful, away from all the stresses and strains of real life."

Scott had invited me here after the incidents with Mark - when I needed to be far, far away from him and anything which could remind me of what had nearly happened. He knew it was a safe house, a retreat. Maybe that explained why he hadn't felt the need to invite anyone there before - no-one else needed rescuing.

"I'm sorry." The words seemed trite, but I didn't know what else to say.

"Don't be." A small smile played on Vivian's lips. "I learned a lot from that marriage and I've not made the same mistake again." She shrugged. "Which is maybe why I don't stay in a relationship where I'm not valued."

Her words hit home. Scott's actions, even though he hadn't followed them up with words, spoke volumes.

My stomach churned. He did care after all.

In spite of the village being fairly small, we both came back with a significant amount of shopping. While I'd paid for most of mine, Vivian had generously bought me a necklace and earring set from one of the boutiques. Even though I'd protested, she'd insisted. Who was I to argue?

By the time we got back to the house, it was starting to get dark.

Vivian excused herself to go to her room.

Bas was in the kitchen, singing badly along to the radio while making a smoothie.

"Want some?" he offered.

The slime green sludge looked about as appetising as cold sick, but he assured me it was full of super foods, all of which would be good for me. I accepted the glass he gave me and tentatively took a sip.

"Oh, you're right. It isn't as bad as it looks at all." I licked my lips, cleaning off the smears left by the kale or spinach or whatever it was.

"Here, you missed a bit." Bas leaned over and smoothed a finger over my bottom lip, lingering for a little longer than necessary.

I sprang back as if I'd been burned, crashing into one of the chairs at the table and bruising my hip. "What do you..." I began.

He held his hands up. "Sorry, I didn't mean anything by it. Don't get freaked out."

Why was it that if anyone who wasn't Scott touched me, I couldn't handle it? Bas's actions were totally innocent, at least I hoped they were.

My phone pinged from my bag - literally saved by the bell. "Thanks for the smoothie, I'll see you later." I backed out of the room and headed upstairs.

Dropping the shopping bags in the middle of the bed, I reached for my phone, seeing the screen had blown up with messages.

Saff: Where the fuck are you?

Saff: What the fuck are you doing with Scott Lincoln?

Saff: Call me as soon as you get this message...

She had also sent through links to various gossip websites which showed me and Scott at the pub the previous evening, and one of us leaving together hand in hand. Unsurprisingly, they speculated as to what we were doing in a country pub, nowhere near either of our homes. It wasn't the first time either of us had been gossip fodder, but I'd thought better of the people who worked in the Kings Arms. If they'd tipped off a pap or even sold the pictures themselves, it was a total betrayal of trust.

Saff answered immediately. She had clearly been waiting for my call.

"Where are you?" she demanded.

"At Scott's mum's house in the country."

"I can see that from the gossip columns. More to the point, what are you doing there? Were you there when we spoke yesterday? Oh my God, Rosie, what's going on?"

I bit my lip, wondering exactly what to tell her. Things had escalated quickly. I guessed Scott hadn't seen any of the pictures, otherwise he'd be in here demanding to know what we should do about them.

"It's complicated," I began.

"Doesn't look like it from those pictures. Looks like you're all loved up with someone who basically treats you like nothing more than a booty call." Saff's anger crackled down the line.

I pulled the phone away from my ear and put Saff on speaker phone so I could examine the pictures in more detail. She was right. To the casual observer, we were like any other couple on a date, laughing at whatever the other one had said, walking close together, holding hands. For every intent and purpose, we were together.

But we weren't.

Two nights didn't suddenly turn us into the new Harry and Meghan.

Vivian's words came back to me. *That's why I don't stay in a relationship where I'm not valued.*

I didn't know my value with Scott, not for sure.

We really did need to talk, to find out what this was going to lead to, if anything.

"Saff, listen, I know what it looks like..."

She berated me again for going back there. But I hadn't been honest with her about the reasons why. "You know what he's like. You saw him when I was on tour with him.

You know what he's capable of doing, making shit up to make him look good and to hell with everyone else. He nearly ruined my relationship with Tris, you know that."

I did. I knew all the reasons why Scott Lincoln didn't make a decent, reliable boyfriend.

I also knew how he made me feel, and I wasn't prepared to deny that.

21

SCOTT

We ended up in the pub again. After a mild family argument about who was going to cook dinner - neither Bas nor I could, Vivian wasn't prepared to, and it wasn't fair to expect Rosie to - it turned out to be the easy option.

There hadn't been a chance to speak with Rosie on her own since she'd come back from her afternoon out with Vivian. I'd have given anything to be a fly on the wall for their conversations. Vivian knew all the dirt in my past, and she wasn't usually backwards in coming forwards when it came to spilling the beans. No wonder Rosie hadn't sought me out straight away when she returned. She hadn't spoken to me on the walk over either, choosing instead to walk with Vivian, leaving me with Bas. It gave me the opportunity to ogle her arse though.

I had to admit she looked absolutely stunning, even dressed down for a country pub. The indigo blue jeans she wore clung to her arse, teamed with a black roll-neck jumper and black heeled boots; simple, yet classic. Her blonde hair was just-rolled-out-of-bed mussed up, and I wanted to pull her in close and take her back to bed.

The landlord greeted Vivian with open arms, gathering her into a hug the moment we walked into the place. "Vivian! How lovely to see you again, I had no idea you were here."

"Gerard, don't tell me such fibs. I was in the village earlier today; I'm sure Marion would have mentioned it."

I rolled my eyes at Bas as they chatted. It had been like this ever since we'd been kids. Gerard flirting with Vivian, pretending his wife hadn't said a word about their glamorous London visitor. You'd have thought after fifteen years they may have tired at the pretence, but apparently not.

"Rosie, what do you want to drink?" Bas asked, making his way to the bar.

She totally ignored me as she pushed past to join Bas. Resting her hands on the bar, she stretched up to look over at the options on the shelves. The motion pushed her cute peachy butt out and I couldn't tear my eyes away. If she carried on like that, I was going to embarrass myself in the middle of the Kings Arms.

"I'll try the rhubarb gin with tonic. Lots of ice please."

"Good choice," agreed Bas. "I'll have the same." He turned to me. "Scott?"

I fucking hated gin. But if it was Rosie's drink of choice this evening, I'd be damned if I'd have anything different. "Yeah, count me in to the gin club. Make mine a double. And I'll have a beer first."

Bas grinned at the bar man. The girl who had served us the previous evening appeared to be absent.

"Easiest round ever, mate. Four rhubarb gins, and a beer for my man."

"Coming right up." He spun away and busied himself making our drinks.

"How was your afternoon with my mum?" asked Bas, leaning back against the bar, angling his body towards Rosie.

Rosie smiled. "Good. Strange at times, but good. She's an interesting woman."

"I have no doubt she regaled you with stories of her past."

"Not to mention stories of *your* past." Rosie cracked a grin.

An unexpected pang of jealousy ripped through me. What had Vivian been telling Rosie about Bas? I didn't like it one bit.

"Here you go." The bar man placed the four balloon glasses down in front of Bas. "Do you want me to start a tab?"

"No, Scott will get this round." Bas gestured to me with his chin as he picked up two of the glasses. "We'll go find a table."

Rosie followed him, carrying the other two glasses, and suddenly I was left on my own. The jealousy gave way to confusion and a simmering anger. How dare he?

The bar man threw open his hands. "Cash or card?"

Stung for the bill, I reached into my jacket and pulled out my wallet.

Vivian appeared next to me. "Let me, darling." She smoothed in and tapped the card machine with her gold card. "What's the matter?"

My gaze found Bas and Rosie, who were chatting animatedly, their heads bent close together.

Vivian looked in the same direction. "Ah, those green eyes are back."

"What are you talking about?"

"You think Bas is making a move on Rosie, and even though you haven't told her how you feel, you don't think he should." Her eyebrows arched as she looked back at me. "Am I right?"

I hated how on the ball she was. How was she able to see everything without me having to say a word? Not to mention how right she was. I let out a hard breath.

"Rosie said you were friends with benefits. Scott, you need to be more than friends with that woman, or you will lose her forever." Vivian brushed a strand of silver hair away from her face. "And you need to do it soon before Sebastian steps in." She glided away towards the table, leaving me alone to contemplate what she'd said.

There was absolutely no doubt she was right.

If I didn't get my act together soon, there would be no hope for me and Rosie.

Sometime later, I swallowed down my fifth double gin and tonic. The more I had, the better they tasted. Unfortunately, they hadn't done much to dull the twinges of envy which pierced my heart every time I looked between Rosie and Bas.

They hadn't done anything more than talk and laugh, with the occasional touch. Bas's hand lingered on Rosie's arm more than once. By the third instance, my foot accidentally slipped under the table and delivered a swift kick to his shin.

"What the fuck, Scott?" His blue eyes bored into mine.

"Sorry, mate," I slurred. "Must have lost my balance."

His mouth twisted into a sneer. "You're sitting down?"

I shrugged and lifted my glass to my mouth again.

"Haven't you had enough tonight?" he asked.

"What are you? My babysitter?" Out of sheer awkwardness, I drained the remainder of the drink and waved the glass in the air. "I think I'll have another."

"Scott, slow down." Rosie warned, her amber eyes fixed on me. "Bas is right, you've had enough."

"Maybe I have had enough," I hissed. "Enough of seeing you flirting with my cousin. Enough of not knowing what we are to each other. Enough of *you*."

She blinked, her lips parting, ready to speak.

Not waiting to hear what would come from her mouth, I cut her off. "Come on, Rosie, why are you really here? We're not in a relationship. You're not my girlfriend. You're not my anything." I echoed the words she'd said to me the first time I rescued her from Mark, wanting to see if she recognised them.

An uncomfortable silence descended over the table. Both Vivian and Bas looked between me and Rosie. I could tell Vivian was itching to say something, but was holding herself back, drumming her fingers on the tabletop instead.

Rosie's blue eyes filled with tears, as she sucked in her bottom lip. "I... you... I," she stuttered, unable to string a coherent sentence together. Without another sound, she pushed her chair back from the table and dashed for the bathrooms.

Vivian glared at me and went after Rosie, leaving Bas and me alone.

I tried to drink some more, but the glass was empty. I struggled to get up. The amount of gin I'd drunk in a short amount of time on an empty stomach, having pushed my dinner around my plate unable to eat, was affecting me more than usual. I knew there was a reason I hated the drink.

"Shit," said Bas, breathing out a long exhalation. "What the hell have you done?"

"What do you care? Oh, wait. Are you going to step in and comfort Rosie after Big Bad Scott told her the truth?" Unable to get the attention of anyone to get me another drink, I reached for Rosie's half empty glass and downed the rest of hers.

"What is the truth though?" His frown deepened. "I know you aren't in a relationship, but it's fucking obvious you both want to be. I can see it, Mum can see it, hell, even the barman can see it!" Bas glanced over in the direction of the Ladies. "You should go and put things right, buddy. Before you fuck everything up for good this time."

"Ha!" I let out a harsh laugh. "Do you think I deserve Rosie after the way I've treated her."

"Maybe you're right and you don't, but if you don't ever take that risk and find out, you'll never know."

Fuck. I hated it when my cousin was right.

But I couldn't talk to her now. I was drunk and angry, the combining state not the best to declare my feelings. Even if I told her the truth now, would she even believe me?

22

ROSIE

S obbing on the shoulder of Vivian Woods in the toilets of the Kings Arms wasn't exactly how I'd expected the evening to pan out.

Watching Scott down drink after drink, descending into the evil version of himself, hearing his cruel words, broke me into a million pieces. I'd thought we'd made some progress, that we were going in the direction of a real relationship. Clearly, I'd got it totally wrong.

"I can't stay." I sniffled into a tissue and pulled away. I couldn't risk ruining Vivian's blouse.

"Don't be ridiculous. Where are you going to go at this time of night?"

"I'll get a train back to London."

Vivian let out a small laugh. "Oh, Rosie, transport links here aren't that good. There won't be a service until the morning."

"I can't go back to the house if he's going to be there."

Right now, the thought of even being in the same postcode as Scott Lincoln made me feel sick. I just wanted to get the hell out of there.

"You can stay in my room, there's a sofa bed I can make up." Vivian rubbed my arm. "You won't have to see him."

My tears started again at her kindness. She'd known me all of a day and was demonstrating more kindness than her nephew, who I had a long history with. A history which apparently meant nothing.

Grateful I'd remembered to bring my handbag, I rifled through the contents to find another tissue to clean my face with. "Can we go home now?"

"Of course, let me go and get my keys." She caught my eye in the mirror. "I won't say anything to Scott."

While I waited, I took several deep breaths, cleaning the streaked mascara from under my eyes. I wanted to get away from here, wanted to get back home.

Back to real life.

These past few days had been like a holiday, a suspended reality; a bubble.

But that bubble had well and truly burst.

Stomped on by Scott.

I hated how easily he'd done it, with only a few words.

Saff had hit the nail on the head with her summation of the situation.

Had Vivian and Bas seen it too?

I felt like a fool for thinking there was more between us.

The door pushed open and Vivian stuck her head in. "We can slip out the back way if you'd like?"

"Perfect," I breathed. "What did Scott say?"

"He wasn't there, he was..." She trailed off.

I didn't need for her to say anything else. I knew he was out there, chatting up some other unsuspecting woman, as if we had never happened. Back to his old ways without even talking to me. I swallowed hard. It couldn't get to me. *He couldn't get to me.* This made his position perfectly clear.

"Let's go."

The hundred hours which followed had me covering an entire gamut of emotions. Vivian had made up the sofa bed in her room, while I collected my stuff from the guest room. I planned on making a getaway as early as possible in the morning. I tossed and turned, unused to sharing a room with someone, waking every time there was an unfamiliar noise. At some point, I heard the front door slam, and some drunken singing. The sounds came close to the door of Vivian's room, but diverted at the last minute. Unsure as to whether it was Scott or Bas, I ended up staying awake, scared one of them was going to come into the room.

When the birds finally started chirruping around half five, I gave up and slipped into the en-suite to get a shower.

The water soothed my fractured thoughts, as I lathered citrus smelling shower gel over my body. The scent was refreshing and uplifting, both of which I needed right now. Once showered and dressed, I re-entered the bedroom. It was empty. After I'd packed the remainder of my things into my suitcase, I perched on the end of the bed and checked my phone for train times.

There was a tentative knock on the door.

I held my breath.

"Rosie?"

"It's okay, Vivian. You can come in, I'm dressed."

She pushed the door open and entered with a tray in her hands. The aroma of pancakes filled the room. My stomach growled. I wasn't sure I could manage to eat anything. Almost as if she could hear my internal thoughts, Vivian spoke.

"I know you probably don't want to eat, but I know what catering on those trains can be like. You'll be eating a fatty bacon sandwich with a million calories and no taste." She smiled as she placed the tray on the dressing table. "This will keep you going."

I couldn't deny they looked amazing. Small and perfectly formed, there was a side of bacon and one of fruit, all topped off with maple syrup. Standing next to the plate was a piping hot cup of coffee.

I couldn't resist. "Thank you." I perched on the stool and began eating, trying to avoid looking at my reflection in the mirror.

"Let me know when you're ready to go. I have a taxi driver on standby for you."

Seriously, she had thought of everything. I wiped a dribble of syrup from my chin. "I can't thank you enough, Vivian. It's been lovely getting to know you."

"And you too, my dear."

"I hope we get to see each other again."

Vivian nodded knowingly. "We will."

I finished my breakfast and drained the last of the coffee. There wouldn't be a decent cup until I got home. Quickly, I went to brush my teeth while Vivian arranged my lift.

"Take care, Rosie," she said, when we were at the front door. "Do let me know you got home safely."

"I will." Impulsively, I pulled her in for a hug. Vivian was probably the best thing to come out of this whole fiasco.

The journey home was fairly uneventful. It being so early, there were several commuters on the train, heads buried in laptops and ereaders or phones. No-one spoke. There was almost a quiet reverence in the carriage. I dozed for a little while, my unsettled night catching up with me.

When I got back to London, the buzz of the city hit me. Even after only a few nights away, the peace and quiet of the countryside now seemed distant. I pushed past the queues, hopped on the Tube and headed back to the sanctuary of my house.

Not bothering to unpack, I stretched out on the sofa, trying to work out how I felt.

A tiny part of me wished I had confronted Scott last night. Although trying to wrangle with a drunk Scott was never easy, let alone when I thought I had something pretty serious I wanted to talk to him about. Maybe I should have persisted instead of running off. He had done the same to me though, so we were even.

And at least now I knew exactly what we were to each other.

Nothing.

Tears formed in the corners of my eyes again. It was pointless getting so upset. Friends with benefits, a hook up, fuck buddy, whatever you wanted to call it.

How was it possible to get upset over something you'd never really had in the first place?

23

SCOTT

G in. Fucking gin.
	Mother's ruin.
	Scott's ruin more like.

Fuck.

I attempted to open my eyes. The pounding in my head certainly wasn't going away anytime soon either.

I deserved every single beat of pain.

Rolling onto my side, I grabbed my phone. The screen was blank and when I pressed the home button, nothing happened. Dead. Like my heart. I fumbled under the bed for the charger and plugged it in.

After a couple of minutes, the screen burst into life. Squinting, I tried to work out what the messages said.

Bas: I'm heading home, doesn't look like you need me as a wing man tonight, lol

Ah, shit. I dragged a hand down my face. The memories of last night were hazy to say the least. The image of Rosie walking away in tears was one I wasn't going to forget in a hurry though. A vague recollection of trying to chat up one of the locals, until her husband arrived, but that was about it. There was no sign of anyone else in the bed or in the room, so it looked likely I had come home alone. How I would explain that to Rosie was a topic for when my brain functioned properly.

Mat: you got any more songs for us? Dec's been working like crazy to come up with something for you.

I sensed there could be a few about heartbreak, if I could be bothered to drag my arse out of bed today. Right now, the prospect of pulling the duvet over my head and ignoring the world was a strong pull.

Saff: We need to talk about you and Rosie. Call me.

I deleted Saff's message straight away. If I didn't have to see it, I didn't have to think about what a complete prick I'd been. How did she know what had happened last night already?

Declan: here you go. Does this work?

He'd attached a sound file and I half-heartedly clicked play.

Soft, acoustic chords came out of the speaker, along with Dec's shit singing voice. He'd taken the chorus I'd sent and worked his magic on it, weaving a melody which rose and fell and built to something epic. Exactly how I'd expected him to, only far, far better.

I sat bolt upright in bed, the sudden movement jarring my brain.

It was absolute fucking perfection.

Imagining it fully mixed and produced brought goose bumps to my skin. I sang along with the track, covering

Dec's atrocious attempts, my voice cracking from lack of sleep and too much alcohol.

A loud knock on the door stopped me in my tracks.

"Hello?" I called. "Come in!"

Vivian appeared in the open doorway, hands on her hips. Even at this hour, she was already dressed, hair and make-up immaculate. Then I realised the hour was close to one in the afternoon, so I shouldn't have been at all surprised.

"Any plans for today?"

Given what Declan had sent me, I wanted to get more of this song down, but I sensed holing up in the cellar wouldn't be the right thing to do.

"I was thinking of taking Rosie out for the afternoon, get some dinner somewhere. Did you want to join us?" I started to throw back the duvet.

"Rosie's not here, Scott." Vivian placed a hand on her hip.

"Oh, did she go into the village again?"

"She left this morning to go back to London."

The thudding in my head which had receded a little came back with vengeance. "She did what?"

"Are you really surprised? After the way you spoke to her last night?"

"I might have had too much to drink." I hung my head.

"Not an excuse, Scott." The way Vivian used my name reminded me of how my mother used to speak to me as a child, normally when I'd done something wrong. Although what I'd done wrong this time was about a million times worse than breaking my great grandmother's precious vase.

I leaped out of the bed.

Vivian shrieked and covered her eyes. "You have to stop doing that! Can you at least wear underwear?"

"Sorry." I grabbed a towel from the chair and wrapped it around my waist. "What time did Rosie leave?"

"I'd give her some time before you go after her. And make sure you know exactly what you want out of it. Don't lead her on, Scott." She turned to leave. "Don't do anything you'll regret later."

Ha. I'd already done that.

After she'd gone, I picked up my phone again. Finding Saff's number, I called her.

"What the hell have you done to Rosie?" she answered without bothering to say hello.

I rubbed my forehead, wincing at her tone. "I got drunk last night and…"

"Last night? I haven't spoken to her since yesterday afternoon when she told me she was staying with you at some family place in the country."

A small wave of relief swept over me. Saff didn't know about last night's episode. Not yet, in any case.

"You know she saw Mark again? And that's why she was with me."

"Mark? Who's Mark?" I could hear the confusion. "She's never mentioned anyone called Mark."

I fell silent. Was it possible Saff wasn't aware what her best friend had been through? Twice? Now I questioned whether it was my place to tell her. If I did, I was breaking Rosie's confidence. Any remaining speck of trust she may have had in me would be blown apart in seconds. I couldn't do that.

"You'll need to ask her, Saff. It's not my business to tell you."

"Whatever it was, it was bad enough that she had to come to you instead of me." Saff blew out a breath. "Can you put her on the phone?"

"I wish I could, but she's not here right now."

"Then get her to call me when she's out of the shower or whatever."

"No, I mean she really isn't here. She's probably back in London by now."

There was a pause. "When you said you got drunk last night?"

I screwed up my eyes. "I was a prick to her."

"Oh, what a surprise. Scott Lincoln fucks it up once again. Will you ever learn?" Saff's disapproval crackled over the line. "I knew those pictures they had of you had to be fake."

"What pictures?"

"She didn't show you the articles on the internet then?"

No, she hadn't. I didn't know anything about any of it. Perhaps if I had, I wouldn't have been such a dick last night.

"Saff, I need to go. I'll catch up with you soon, yeah?" Before she had the chance to say anything else, I cut the call.

Firing up a browser, I typed my name and Rosie's into a search bar. Within seconds, I'd found the article Saff must have been referring to. It showed us in the pub the other night, pictures of us at our table, laughing together, and one of us leaving together holding hands. My blood ran cold.

Every other time I'd stayed here, the locals respected my privacy, never took advantage of having an up and coming rock star in their presence. The minute I arrive with a well-known model, all bets appeared to be off.

Seeing how happy we looked together stung. Had it only been two nights ago we'd been so into each other?

No matter what my mouth had said, my heart thought otherwise.

I'd been a complete idiot.

24

ROSIE

"Surprise!" Ellie's voice crackled through the intercom when I answered it. "I'm in town for a meeting and thought we could catch up."

I hesitated. Since coming back from the country, I'd hibernated in my house for two days, barely leaving it. Getting dressed was a distant memory. I'd thrown a baggy tracksuit over my sleep clothes, before moving from bed to couch. An episode of the Kardashians froze on the television screen, while I answered the door.

"Um, I've not really been well," I mumbled. "Might not be such a good idea for you to come in."

"Bollocks. I can't stay too long anyway, gotta get over to Shoreditch by three." Ellie explained. "I've got the final pictures from the shoot."

My heart sank. The last thing I needed was a reminder.

"Please, Rosie? Plus, I'm dying for a pee."

Reluctantly, I pressed the buzzer to let her in, and wedged the front door open. Not two minutes later, she burst in, thrust her bags at me and rushed into the bathroom.

"Thanks! Won't be a minute."

I dumped her things onto the armchair and resumed my place on the sofa. My hand hovered over the remote to restart the programme, but I thought better of it and turned it to a music channel instead. Immediately, I wished I hadn't. They were playing one of Trash Gun's most popular tracks. Scott's face filled the screen, and I stared at it, unable to breathe.

"Ooo, how's Scott?" asked Ellie, coming back into the living room. "You mentioned you'd seen him?"

Defiantly, I changed the channel again, and tossed the remote aside. "He's a prick."

"I know that. But you two?"

"We're nothing." Saying the words out loud hammered home the message he'd given me. It hurt like hell, but I couldn't do anything to change the situation. I had to pretend I was fine with it. "You said you had the *SFU* images?"

"Yeah." Ellie sank into the armchair and wrestled with her portfolio to show me. "The chemistry in some of those shots with Mark is off the scale."

My hand froze in mid-air as I went to take the folder from her. With everything which had gone on with Scott, I'd almost - almost - forgotten about Mark. I wrestled with myself, debating whether to tell Ellie. I knew she had my back and if, for one moment, she thought he'd be damaging to her brand, she'd pull the campaign.

"Great, can't wait to see them." I forced myself to

examine the photos. Looking at the shots, I could see what she meant. It looked like we were close and intimate, a couple. All the things he'd wanted, but not in a normal way. I couldn't let him try to do it to anyone else. "Ellie, there's something I need to tell you about Mark..."

Fifteen minutes later, the entire shoot had been ripped to shreds and shoved into my kitchen bin. Ellie went absolutely ballistic, calling Mark every name under the sun and swearing he would never work in the industry again. When I told her about the *Aspire* casting, she immediately called the fashion director and told her the truth.

She really was a brilliant friend.

"Thank fuck we hadn't released any of this yet."

A lump formed in my throat. "Ellie, I sent Scott a couple of the pictures by accident."

"Of you? Or of both of you?"

"Only me. It was the lingerie ones."

Ellie waved her hand. "He can keep them to wank over. I wouldn't want to destroy his fantasies."

I doubted his fantasies would feature me right now, but I was grateful I didn't have to approach him about getting them back. "What are you going to do about the range now?"

Ellie sucked in her bottom lip. "We can't move the go live date, but I really want to get some promo done. We can reshoot you easily, but I need a male model. Someone you're comfortable working with." She tapped her phone against her thigh. "Someone trustworthy. And hot." The corner of her mouth quirked up.

An idea popped into my head. The person I had in mind

wasn't exactly trustworthy. Scott would despise it. "I think I might know someone…"

Which is how, two days later, Bas Rafferty and I ended up in the penthouse suite of a West London hotel, recreating the original *SFU* shoot.

When I'd asked him, he'd initially refused. Laughing, he told me he wasn't a model and had never harboured any aspirations to get his top off for public consumption. I knew he was lying. I'd seen his previous work. Ellie also spoke to him, persuading him it was for the greater good, although she didn't go into detail about why the first shoot had got canned. I wasn't about to enlighten him either.

"Shit, I can see what Scott sees in you." Bas raked his gaze over my near naked body, as we prepped for the lingerie pictures.

Instinctively, I reached for a robe and pulled it on. I didn't like to think that the two of them had discussed me in such intimate detail. Heat rushed to my cheeks.

As if sensing my discomfort, Bas went on. "Not that he's ever said anything about, well, you know. I can make my own decisions when it comes to seriously fantastic looking women."

For the duration of the shoot, Ellie was never far away, making sure there was always someone else around me and Bas. She needn't have worried; he was a perfect gentleman. When his fingers brushed against my hipbone, I couldn't help but compare him to Scott. His skin was smoother, unblemished by tattoos, and it was obvious he kept himself in shape. He moved and posed easily, taking direction well, making me feel at ease. The experience couldn't have been more different, and it brought out the best in me as well.

When Ellie finally told us it was a wrap, applause broke out from the small group of people who'd put the shoot together.

"Seriously, Bas, you ought to get Rosie to hook you up with her booker." Ellie came over to us, handing me a robe. "That face could make you a fortune."

He laughed as I slipped on the robe. "I'm doing a favour for a friend. Happy to help out." He flashed a smile in my direction.

"Sure I can't get you to change your mind?" pressed Ellie. "Over a drink?"

My head swivelled around to her. "Ellie!"

"What? A girl can ask, right?" She threw her hands in the air. "Okay, I get it, you want him all to yourself. Can't say I blame you."

"Rosie?" Bas's tone lowered and he fixed me with a look, reminiscent of the ones Scott used to give me.

"No, that's not what I meant at all!" I protested. "Why don't the three of us go out afterwards?"

"I forgot. I'm getting a train straight back to Manchester." Ellie turned away and pretended there was something on her phone which was imperative she looked at immediately. I wondered if she was booking her train, so as not to deal with the awkwardness in the room.

After Ellie had left, Bas and I ended up in the hotel bar. It was quiet. There were a few tables occupied by people in suits, either catching up after work or having business meetings. Bas ordered my gin and his pint, and we occupied a table to the side of the room, out of the earshot of others.

"Have you spoken to Scott?" Bas asked.

I sipped my drink. I hadn't heard from him since I'd left the country house. Nothing in almost a week. Several times I'd picked up my phone, ready to call or message him. Then I remembered it shouldn't be up to me to make contact.

He was the one who had pissed on whatever it was we had.

Shat on any kind of feelings I harboured for him.

I squashed those feelings down hard.

Didn't want to let myself drown in the weight of rejection.

"No. Have you?"

Bas twisted his pint glass around, avoiding my gaze. "I think he's back home now. He didn't stay at the house for long after you'd left."

"That's not a surprise. He was only meant to be there for a week. The band were going into the studio when he got back.".

"Yeah, he said something along those lines." He fixed me with a stare. "What's going on with you two? Are you together?"

"We've never been together," I snapped. "At least, not in any kind of long-term relationship. It doesn't suit either of us."

"You're a shit liar, Rosie Tatton." The corner of Bas's mouth curled up. "And, unfortunately, so is Scott."

25

SCOTT

"Fuck's sake, Declan. Play the chords softer, it doesn't need to drown out the drums." I stalked across the studio floor, tapping my fingers against my thighs.

Declan glared at me. "I was playing it softer."

"Then try again."

I stopped at the refreshments table, debating whether it was too early for a beer. Eleven o'clock said it wasn't. The way the others were sending furious glances my way confirmed it was. Reluctantly, I poured myself a coffee, cheersing the guys with my mug and a sarcastic smile.

The shitty mood I'd been in started the minute Rosie had left. Knowing her departure was all my own doing made it worse. I hadn't mustered up the courage to contact her, so I hadn't apologised or put things right between us again yet.

If only I'd be honest with my feelings, instead of using alcohol to avoid them.

Bas had berated me for days, telling me what an idiot - and some other choice words - I'd been. He'd spotted the connection between us. One reason, he said, why he hadn't made a move himself. Now there was no reason for him not to.

I rolled my head around, trying to stretch out my neck. The tension in my shoulders meant they were up near my ears.

The creativity which had been bursting out of me while I'd taken a break, had all but disappeared. All the songs I'd written were shit. Nothing but a bunch of word vomited meaningless passages.

Especially the one for Rosie.

We were trying to get the bare bones of the song down, but I picked holes in everything: Dec's bridge, Mat's bass line, Bobby's timing. I couldn't bring myself to sing it either. Every word burned.

"Seriously, Scott. Can you just piss off and let us get on with it?" suggested Mat. "Let us get the music sorted on our own, then you can see what we've done. Being a stubborn and grumpy bastard isn't really helping."

I crossed my arms over my chest. Part of me knew he was absolutely right. Giving them some space to work things out, like I usually would, made sense. But the stubborn and grumpy bastard in me rose his head. "Why? I'll still hate whatever you've come up with, so I may as well stay around."

Mat sank back in his chair and let out a hard breath. "You wanna try another song?"

"Might as well. This isn't working."

We flicked through the new material, and I selected a song which I knew would better suit my current mindset. An earthy, raw, punk driven set of lyrics needing driving riffs and hard-hitting rhythm sections.

I hummed the idea of the tune to Declan and Mat, while Bobby listened in, drumming a potential beat with his fingers.

The angry, belligerent nature of this particular song soothed my mood, channelling my negative energy in a better way. I screamed out one of the verses and my frustrations slipped from my body, leaving in their place not exactly a calm, but an acceptance of things I couldn't control.

"You reckon you can replicate that on stage?" Mat raised an eyebrow, as he observed me coughing and panting with exertion.

"Of course." I didn't bat an eyelid. "Reckon the front row will be begging for it."

He rolled his eyes. "Didn't think you needed the audience anymore."

"What do you mean?"

"You and Rosie Tatton. Thought you two were serious after that pic last week of you at the country pile."

All the good work done by the punk song dissipated after Mat mentioned Rosie's name.

"Fuck off," I growled, throwing a cushion at his face.

He laughed and chucked it back at me. "Hit a nerve, did I?"

They knew me better than I knew myself.

I flopped down onto the floor, lying on my back and staring at the ceiling. "What have we got for the album then?" Focus. If I could get some focus back, I might be able to get all thoughts of Rosie out of my head.

Declan dropped a whole ream of paper onto my chest. "Enough for a double-triple-special-edition if this is anything to go by. You really did manage to get some work done while you were away shagging Rosie."

"Don't talk about her like that!" I sat up abruptly, the pages scattering around my body. "In fact, don't ever talk about her again. Any of you!" Hauling myself to my feet, I slammed out of the studio in the direction of the kitchen.

There was no-one else there, none of the studio staff or any of the visiting mixers and producers. I relished the solitude to straighten out my head and clear my thoughts.

Working on new stuff with the band always had potential tipping points. We were close, more than close, always had been. Wouldn't have been able to spend so much time together without driving each other totally crazy. But sometimes, just sometimes, someone would overstep a mark. And that mark had to do with Rosie right now.

I pulled out my phone and opened up the messaging app.

It should be so easy to apologise.

To tell her how you really feel, the voice in my head whispered.

Ugh. Fuck. I hated this.

I wished I could go back to the pub, not get so fucked up

on gin and pretend in front of Vivian and Bas that Rosie meant nothing to me.

Any kind of inspiration for an apology deserted me and I stared at the blank screen, willing some words of wisdom to come.

The door creaked behind me. I shoved my phone back in my pocket, turning to see Mat entering the room.

"You okay?"

"You have to ask?" I itched to light a cigarette, but the warning posters on the walls plus the smoke detector in plain sight advised against it.

"Ignore Dec. He's a dickhead sometimes."

I sniggered. "Most of the time, to be fair."

Mat busied himself making a coffee. "Want one?"

"Sure. Considering you won't let me have beer."

"Touché." He heaped the coffee into a mug. "And you'll be on a caffeine high now instead. As if it isn't bad enough with your nervous energy anyway."

"Who knows? We might get everything down this afternoon." I did a stupid dance, ending up with jazz hands.

"Unlikely if you stay in this mood." Mat passed me the drink. "What is going on with you and Rosie then?" He held up his hands. "You don't have to tell me if you don't want to."

My mood dipped. Mat was a good friend. I knew he wasn't digging for the sake of it. He wanted to know what was going on for the overall good of the band. But if I told him how I felt about Rosie, it would be out there, and then I couldn't take it back.

"Nothing," I said, letting out a hard breath. "There's

nothing going on. You know the history we've got. It hasn't changed."

"Not a bad history to have though. She is smoking." He winked.

I had a funny feeling our history might be all we turned out to have.

26

ROSIE

"Excuse the mess. Tris is being a typical builder and putting his clients before his own house." Saff ushered me in through the front door of their new house, the hallway of which was cluttered with paint tins, offcuts of wood, boxes of flat pack furniture and a roll of carpet.

"Oy, I heard that!" Tris called from the living room. "Can I help it Col became a decorator to the stars after doing your brother's place?"

She directed me to the kitchen. "This is the only room that's really sorted. Ironic as we mostly get takeout."

The small room at the back of the house overlooked the garden, a strip of grass with a patio and space for a table and chairs. Functionally kitted out with the usual appliances and decorated in a muted yet warm mushroom colour, it screamed cosy and traditional - the exact opposite of Saff.

"Wine?" she asked, reaching into the fridge for an unopened bottle.

"Please." I sat down at the table and dropped my bag on the floor beside me.

She sloshed the wine into two large glasses and passed one to me. "So. I haven't seen you since Brixton, but it seems I've missed out on a hell of a lot of gossip. You wanna tell me about it?"

I lifted the glass to my lips and took a large slug. "Not really. There's nothing to tell."

Her eyes narrowed as she sipped her own drink. "You and Scott in a cosy country hideaway and there's nothing to tell? I call bullshit."

"Do you see him here?" I gestured around the room with my glass. "Is he by my side when I'm coming over to dinner with my best friend?"

"Um, he lives in Manchester?"

"Details, Saff, details. If there was anything between us, he'd be here, I'm sure of it." I gulped down more wine, needing the alcohol to loosen my tongue and bring out the real truth.

The doorbell rang, and Saff yelled out to Tris to answer it.

I guessed it was whatever food we were having tonight. Mumbled voices came from the hallway and the door slammed shut. Expecting Tris to appear with the bags, my jaw dropped as he arrived in the kitchen with another guy.

"Hey, Rosie." Tris came over and hugged me. "This is Andy. He's one of my mates from home." He jerked his thumb in the direction of the dark-haired chap standing behind him.

My head snapped around to Saff. "What's he doing here?" I mouthed.

"We arranged it ages ago." Saff wasn't so bothered about keeping my discomfort from Andy. "Double date kind of thing." She waved her wine glass around as if that explained everything.

Honestly, I couldn't remember agreeing to it. Judging by Andy's bugged out eyes, I wasn't sure he had either.

Tris went to the fridge and grabbed two bottles of beer, opening them both and passing one to Andy. He downed almost half of it in one go, gulping hard.

"Nice to meet you, Rosie." He swiped a hand across his mouth, before holding it out to me.

"Er, you too?" I glanced between his hand and Saff, who was trying not to laugh.

The guys sat down at the table, and we made polite conversation while we waited for the food. Saff stopped asking about Scott, choosing instead to focus on how single and available I was. Andy barely said a word while he listened, knocking back beer as if it were water. The same could be said about me and the wine.

Around fifteen minutes later, we were saved by the bell - literally.

Saff and Tris went to the door leaving me and Andy alone.

"Do you want another drink?" He stood up.

"Sure, thanks." I glanced around the kitchen. "I guess I could find some plates and cutlery." While he refilled our drinks, I opened cupboards and drawers until I got what I was looking for. I could feel Andy watching me, and I wasn't

sure whether to be flattered or alarmed. Poor guy had probably been expecting a fun night with a supermodel - ha -
and he'd ended up with me, pining after a rock star. Even if
nothing came of it, I should at least make some sort of effort.

During dinner, I did exactly that.

We feasted on crispy prawns, chilli squid, gyoza, katsu
curry and ramen noodles, washed down with more beer and
wine.

"There's a great Japanese restaurant in Soho, have you
been?" Andy asked, waiting to see if I wanted the last duck
gyoza. "What am I saying? Of course you would have!"

"Which one?" I stuck a fork into the little dumpling and
lifted it to my mouth. I might have been well-travelled and
seen a number of cultures, but I still couldn't use chopsticks
to save my life.

He named a place I had visited on a number of
occasions.

"Yes! I love it there, it's so reminiscent of one I went to in
New York."

"Did you go to Mr Taka Ramen when you were there?"

"The Time Out Market is amazing!"

Saff and Tris watched on with interest as we bantered
back and forth about New York and various restaurants and
bars we'd been to. Andy was definitely a foodie, which
surprised me. I guess I shouldn't have been so dismissive of
him at the start. While we chatted, I didn't feel any physical
kind of attraction to him though. He didn't make my skin
prickle if he glanced in my direction. Not like a certain
someone who I didn't want to think about right now.

Once we'd finished dessert, Saff jumped up from the

table. "Come on, let's get a photo to show how domesticated I've become."

"You're joking, right?" Tris rolled his eyes at Saff's suggestion.

"No, it'll be fun." Saff fiddled about with her phone, setting up the timer and getting us into position.

"Are you sure you want me in it?" Andy asked, nervously edging to one side out of the way.

"Yes, come on, how often do you get to have your picture taken with a rock star and a supermodel?" Tris joked.

I beckoned him over to sit beside me and leaned into him. "Just pretend the photographer's naked, that's what I do," I whispered in his ear, before placing a gentle kiss on his cheek as the picture got taken.

He stiffened beside me. I drew back and picked up my glass, winking at him. We raised our drinks to the camera, as ever wondering if any of the shots would actually work out. After a few attempts, Saff went to check them.

"Seriously, I have a double chin in that one!" I covered my face.

Andy leaned over my shoulder, peering at the picture. "I honestly don't see it. You look perfect."

I turned to one side, breathing in his aftershave. "You don't have to say that."

He stared deeply into my eyes, lost in a moment which only he seemed to be involved in.

"Rosie, you can have the final editorial say." Saff thrust her phone in front of us, oblivious to what might have been happening. "Pick the best one."

Reluctantly, I took it from her and swiped through the

pictures, deleting the ones which I hated. No matter what Andy had said, I still didn't like looking at myself. "Any of those will do." I handed the device back to her, watching as she uploaded them to her socials.

All too soon, Andy said he had to go to catch the last train home.

We'd had fun, chatting about New York and other travel locations we had in common. I felt relaxed in his company, but there was something missing.

When he touched my arm, or brushed my hair away from my face, I didn't *feel* anything.

Not like I did when Scott did the same thing.

"Can I get your number?" Andy asked, shifting from foot to foot as he stood up.

No! My heart screamed.

"Sure, give me your phone." I smiled politely and held out my hand. I tapped in a number and passed it back to him.

Saff watched me with narrowed eyes. "Good to see you again, Andy. Looks like we might see a bit more of you."

"Hope so." Andy leaned down and kissed me on both cheeks. "I'll be in touch."

"Let me see you out." Tris walked out into the hallway with him.

Inwardly, I let out a sigh of relief, masking it from Saff. "He seems like a nice guy.".

"He is. A genuine guy who was there for Tris when he needed someone the most."

A tiny pang of guilt hit me in the stomach. I'd changed a

digit on the phone number I'd put into Andy's phone. He wouldn't be able to contact me directly.

Why had I been such a bitch?

Because, in spite of everything, Scott Lincoln was still the one I wanted.

27

SCOTT

W ho the fuck was @andy_b_morse57_ and what the hell was he doing with Rosie?

My eyes narrowed as I scrutinised the picture in more detail.

Saff and Tris were also there, possibly in their new house.

It appeared to be the epitome of a cosy, double date dinner.

Everything I would usually be repelled by.

But the fact it was Rosie, with someone who wasn't me, had my green eyes out in force yet again.

On closer inspection, it all appeared quite innocent, although I didn't like the way Rosie's lips were grazing this Andy's cheek. Or the way he had his hand on her thigh.

Jealousy burned like a bitch.

Boredom also made me edgy.

With no gigs planned, and studio time the only outlet

for my nervous energy, sitting around my apartment night after night was starting to take its toll.

It might have been close to ten o'clock, but the lure of a bar was strong. The Matchbox wasn't far, practically my local. I'd been going there almost my entire life, as soon as I was old enough to drink, not to mention several times before. They'd welcome me with open arms. I might even catch the end of a gig.

Ripped and baggy track pants, teamed with a similarly distressed vest didn't cut it for leaving the house. I stepped into the bedroom and found a pair of skinny jeans, I threw them on and grabbed a black buttoned shirt, shoving my feet into a pair of boots. I grabbed my phone and wallet, slipped on a jacket and left the flat.

Walking to the club, I fished out a cigarette and lit it, the plumes of smoke rising in the chilly air. There were a few people around, mostly finishing their night rather than starting it like I was. I walked past unnoticed and unrecognised.

The bouncer at the door of The Matchbox nodded to me and let me straight in.

Music assaulted my ears. A band I didn't know.

It always gave me a buzz: seeing someone who could potentially support Trash Gun on future tours; spotting the budding talents of a young, up and coming group.

Entering the main body of the place, it surprised me to see it only half full. Clearly the band in question didn't have a big fan base. I headed to the bar, finding a stool at the end where I could drink undisturbed, but still see the stage.

The bar manager placed a tumbler of whisky in front of me. "On the house, Scott. Good to see you again. You come to check out the band?" He nodded to the stage, where the lead singer encouraged the small audience to sing along to their song.

I shrugged noncommittally. It hadn't been my intention to see the band, they were a pleasant distraction though.

"They're not all that great." He carried on cleaning glasses as he chatted. "You can see there's not a crowd like the last time you were in. But they're local lads, and you know I always like to give them a break."

My attention diverted to the stage, and I watched the band with a critical eye this time. There were four of them, all guys, the lead singer also playing guitar. Declan would kill me if I tried to take that away from him. I let him have the glory, my guitar tekkers weren't up there with his. Similar to me, the singer also wasn't blessed with good skills. It detracted from his singing and overall stage presence, he spent much too much time looking at his fingers on the fretboard rather than connecting with the audience. The lead guitarist was strong, as was the drummer, but the bassist let the side down. Ha, if I ever thought of giving up on the performance side, I could always make it as a talent spotter for a label. I chuckled at the thought, slugging down the whisky and gesturing for another.

"What do you think?" A female voice close to my ear whispered just loud enough to be heard over the noise.

I turned to see a gorgeous brunette, with sparkling brown eyes standing next to me, sucking on the straw poking out of her drink. Dressed in a black mini skirt, patterned vest top and a choker around her neck, she was on the wrong side of skinny for me. I preferred my women with a few more curves, although I didn't instantly dismiss her.

"They're okay." I hedged my bets on the side of neutral. Too often in the past I'd fallen foul of the same question, only to be chastised by the singer's girlfriend-slash-manager-slash-sister.

"Really? You think?" Her eyebrows raised. "Personally, I think they're weak. No Trash Gun, obviously." The corner of her mouth quirked, those brown eyes full of mischief.

I wasn't sure whether to be flattered or terrified she knew who I was. Crazy stalker fans didn't do it for me either.

"You with the band?" I asked, to be sure.

"Fuck no!" She laughed. "I'm staying with my sister for a few days. She's boring as hell though, so I snuck out for some fun."

Convenient...

"Sounds familiar." I grinned. "Then shall we have some fun together?"

Twenty minutes later, Amy and I were in one of the VIP booths, sitting opposite each other. The drinks were free-flowing, a bottle of whisky had appeared and all I had to do was pour my own shots. Amy was drinking vodka and tonics, four glasses lined up ready to be consumed. She appeared to be able to hold her liquor pretty well. Easy to talk to, I'd discovered she was still at university studying media communications. Her parents had wanted her to do something more meaningful, like her sister who was studying medicine. Slightly nervous that her choice of university subject might make me a project for her, I'd kept most of my answers to her questions short and to the point. Never give too much away. You never know who might be listening. After the fiasco with Saff on tour and the recent faux pas with Rosie, I'd learned that lesson.

Her fingers snaked across the table to stroke my knuckles. "You're nothing like I'd expected."

"You know the media doesn't always get it right," I teased, enjoying the feel of her skin on mine.

"I'm not seeing the arrogant, full of himself, confident prick who struts about a stage, giving girls their first orgasm with only a look." Amy's lips closed over the straw in her drink and immediately I thought how they might look wrapped around my cock.

"Is that your kind of guy?" I leaned back in my seat, pulling my hand away. "Arrogant?"

She ran her tongue around her lips. "I prefer the term alpha."

My eyes not leaving hers, I lifted my glass to my mouth and swallowed a large mouthful of alcohol. I deserved some fun.

Back in my flat, it appeared my mind and my heart were at loggerheads with one another.

Amy wandered around examining my few meagre possessions, pointing at the gold records on the wall and asking questions. Her level of nosiness began to grate. She wanted to know about everything. The nagging thought in the back of my mind questioned her motives. A media communications student hanging out with a notorious 'bad boy' who wasn't far from the gossip columns? The back of my neck prickled.

"Do you want a drink?" I leaped up from the chair and went to the kitchen. "I've got some vodka here somewhere."

She tossed back her hair and stared at me through narrowed eyes. "I've had enough to drink. I thought we were going to have some fun?" Amy pouted, and settled down on the sofa, patting the seat next to her.

My dick twitched uncomfortably. I couldn't deny she was good looking, but I was having trouble putting my finger on why I didn't want to leap into bed with her. The potential kiss and tell aspect was only one reason. There was something else.

Almost against my better judgement, I went to join Amy. As soon as I'd sat down, she swung her legs and straddled me, tiny breasts pressing against my chest, skirt riding up her thighs. Instinctively, I grabbed her arse, controlling her movements. If she wanted alpha...

Her lips landed on mine, tongue slipping into my mouth, hands gripping my shoulders to steady herself.

I tried to respond, tried to get into the moment with her.

It wasn't the fact she might sell her story of her night with me which bothered me the most.

It was simpler than that.

She wasn't Rosie Tatton.

Fuck. Fuck. Fuck.

"Wait, stop," I murmured against her lips.

When she continued, I grasped her shoulders and pushed her away.

"I'm sorry. You need to go."

Her blue eyes clouded over. "What do you mean? I thought you wanted this?"

"I thought I did too, but..." My voice trailed off. What could I tell her? That I was in love with someone who I'd pushed away because I *was* that arrogant, full of himself, confident prick Amy had described? I was too scared to even admit it to myself, let alone anyone else.

"Fine. Whatever." Her tone changed, harsher now. She extricated herself from our position and grabbed her bag. "I thought you were going to be different. Guess you're like all the rest." Without saying another word, she slammed out of the flat leaving me alone.

I reached for my phone and fired up the picture Rosie posted earlier. She looked happy. @andy_b_morse57_ looked like the kind of guy who wouldn't fuck around with her feelings, like I had.

28

ROSIE

When my phone rang with an unknown number, I almost didn't answer it. I hadn't been involved in an accident, PPI claims were a thing of the past and all my insurances were up to date. Mentally preparing myself for a conversation with a cold caller, I accepted the call. "Hello?"

"Rosie? It's Vivian Woods."

The last person I'd expected to get a call from was Scott's aunt. "Vivian, hi, how are you?"

"I hope you don't mind me contacting you, my dear. I got your number from Sebastian. Although I still can't get used to seeing him all over the internet in just his pants." She chuckled. "And you look lovely in those pictures too, such a healthy role model."

"Thank you, and of course I don't mind." I muted the television, giving Vivian my full attention.

"I wondered if you might be free to meet for afternoon tea later today."

My schedule yawned with the emptiness of it. I was waiting to hear back on a lot of castings and possible interviews, but I was certainly available that afternoon. "I'd love to, where do you want to meet?"

She gave me the name of a French cafe, which specialised in patisserie, on Kensington High Street.

"Sounds perfect. I'll see you there at three?"

"Splendid. I look forward to seeing you later."

My face wrinkled with curiosity after we said our goodbyes. Now what could Vivian Woods possibly want?

I tapped my phone against my chin, then called Bas.

"Why does your mum want to have afternoon tea with me?" I demanded the minute he answered.

"Hi Bas, how are you doing? I'm good thanks, Rosie. How are you?"

"Sorry," I sighed. "It seemed a bit suspicious, that's all."

"Since you were at the house, she's barely talked about anyone else. I think she's worried about you."

His words stopped me in my tracks. The last thing I'd expected was for Vivian to care about me. After all, we'd spent less than a couple of days together and I'd probably left attractive snot marks on one of her best outfits.

"Really?"

"Yes, really. It's almost as if she wants to adopt you or something. Then I can carry on being the black sheep of the family." He laughed. "She really loves our *SFU* campaign, though."

The images had gone viral and blown up in a big way. Both Ellie and I were grateful to Bas for stepping in. Funny how things turned out.

"Although not so keen on seeing you in your pants, apparently." I paused and gnawed on the edge of my thumb nail. "So you think this afternoon tea is more of a getting to know you thing?"

"Yep, definitely. Takes the heat off of me. You two have fun now. I want to hear all about it when we next meet."

We made some vague plans to catch up and then ended the call.

I changed my outfit around three times before settling on something which I thought would be appropriate. It was almost worse than getting ready for a first date.

With the amount of charity work Vivian got involved in, I admired her. I remembered doing a catwalk show for one of the homeless charities she supported, which ended up raising thousands of pounds from the auction of the clothes afterwards. Not to mention the dinner for domestic abuse survivors. She was an eminent woman, quietly supporting a number of worthy causes without getting too much attention herself. I wondered how influential she'd been in Scott's upbringing.

Ugh. Scott. I'd been doing a pretty good job of not thinking about him recently. Saff kept going on at me to go on a proper date with Andy, but I couldn't. I didn't want to lead the poor guy on when I knew it wouldn't go anywhere.

I needed a friend with benefits.

Perhaps it was time to move on.

The little French cafe was quietly buzzing when I arrived, and I scanned the tables for Vivian. She waved at me from a table in the back and I made my way over to her.

Vivian stood as I got to the table and air kissed me on both cheeks. "You look lovely," she cooed.

Grateful I'd taken some time in choosing my outfit, I'd finally settled on a mid-length pleated leopard print skirt, biker boots, a black polo neck and leather biker's jacket. It appeared the right mix of casual and smart.

"You too." I stepped back and admired her Pucci print shift dress and navy kitten heels. Classic, timeless, elegant. Gah. I think I wanted to be Vivian Woods when I grew up.

"How are you doing?" Vivian asked when we'd sat down.

I pretended to study the menu. "I'm okay."

She reached across the table and rested her hand on mine. "If it's any consolation, I'm fairly sure Scott feels the same."

"He's not even tried to contact me. I doubt that very much," I snorted.

"The two of you would make a great couple." A smile tugged at her lips. "Beautiful babies."

Before I could respond, the maitre'd appeared to take our order. Vivian had promised afternoon tea, and ordered the works, including a bottle of champagne as well as tea. After what she'd just suggested, I definitely needed a drink.

"Sebastian said you were wondering why I'd asked to meet you." Vivian took a sip of her champagne, while I downed half a glass.

"Well, yes. I'm sorry if that sounds weird."

"Not at all, I appreciate we don't really know each other that well, and the invitation must have come out of the blue." She smoothed a hand over her perfectly styled grey hair. "I wasn't joking about you and Scott, although that wasn't the reason for wanting to see you."

The cake stand with its tiny, precisely cut sandwiches, the macarons, and the scones arrived. I hadn't been eating a great deal recently, but now I was starving. Somehow, stuffing my face with small but perfectly formed food seemed the right thing to do. It also got the subject away from Scott.

"I'm hosting a charity dinner next Tuesday, and I'd be delighted if you would be able to come along." Vivian took her time in selecting a few things from the stand, while my stomach growled in anticipation. "It's for a good cause."

I didn't doubt that. Anything Vivian got involved with would be a worthy enterprise. "Of course, I'd be happy to come. Which charity are you supporting?"

"It's for homeless and missing persons. After my first marriage ended, Sebastian and I spent a little time sofa surfing, as it's called these days. After I'd exhausted the hospitality of my friends and family, we didn't have a place of our own to live for months. Now I'm in a position to do so, I want to be able to give back and help people who are in a similar situation."

Her confession floored me. I remembered Scott telling me the country house was the product of a divorce settlement, but I hadn't realised how much she'd struggled previously. To have come out of something like that with such grace and poise impressed me even more.

"Wow, that's incredible." I blinked. "I had no idea."

"It's not something I tell everyone, Rosie. But I thought it might help you to understand a little more about me." The corner of her mouth curled up. "It's not all glamour and parties for the sake of it, you know."

A laugh escaped my lips. "Oh, I know. Sometimes putting up a front helps."

"Talking of which, have you told Scott how you really feel about him?" Vivian took a bite from a macaron.

"How I...?" My voice trailed off. Of course I hadn't. I tried to force down those emotions and had ignored the way he'd been so protective of me, scooped me up and taken me away from it all. It all seemed like a distant memory now. Those two days of unadulterated bliss, being together, away from all the stress and pressure now seemed like a different life. A different world. I gulped down more champagne, trying to deflect the question. But this was Vivian, it wasn't Saff, or Ellie I felt I owed it to her to be honest.

Taking a deep breath, I answered. "I can't, Vivian. He's made it blatantly clear he's not interested. Why would I put myself through that?"

Vivian sipped her tea, a thoughtful expression crossing her face. "Don't be too sure, my dear. And if you do have feelings for him, don't leave it until it's too late to tell him."

29

SCOTT

I hadn't been out in days. Ever since the fiasco with Amy and finding out Rosie was seeing some guy called Andy, I festered in my apartment. I called for takeout if I was hungry, got the basics delivered in an online food shop, and basically drank or smoked my way through the long, long hours. Mat, Declan and Bobby had called and messaged, but I ignored them. They'd been working hard in the studio getting down the musical background to the new songs, waiting for me to come and put vocals over the top. I'd left them to it, not exactly being in the right frame of mind to observe and critique appropriately. Deep buried anger and resentment didn't make me an impartial observer right now.

In the middle of the rerun of Top Gear I'd become addicted to, my phone vibrated. As usual, I gave it a cursory glance, intending to disregard whoever was bothering me this time.

Mat: I'm coming over whether you like it or not. Make sure you're dressed and not wanking when I get there.

It was as if he could see me stretched out on the sofa in skanky boxer shorts and a vest top which had seen better days. Yeah, I'd had my hand down my shorts at times, but Matt LeBlanc didn't do it for me.

I rested my head back against the cushion and stared up at the ceiling. I could tell him not to bother, but he'd come over anyway. Reluctantly, I unlocked my phone and fired back a response.

Scott: Ring when you're ten minutes away so I can clear away the tissues.

Mat sent back a laughing emoji and a thumbs up.

I dragged myself off the couch and into the bathroom. My reflection stared back at me: blood shot eyes, dark circles, a jawline darkened by unkempt stubble. Honestly, I looked like shit, with no-one to blame but myself. I stripped off my vest and shorts, nose wrinkling at the smell as I tossed them into the corner. No surprise really, I couldn't remember the last time I'd showered.

The powerful jets of the shower went some way to washing away the stench of despair and loneliness, along with the fresh lemony scent of the shower gel. Scrubbing away what felt like layers of grime and dirt, my mood began to improve. I really hadn't appreciated the feel-good factor of being fresh and clean.

Once dressed in jeans and a clean t-shirt, I pulled open the blinds, blinking as the weak sunshine streamed through the large windows.

The phone rang. I pounced on it, seeing Mat's name on the screen. I answered, putting him on speaker. "Hey, mate."

"I'm ten minutes away. Hope you're not still in your pants." I could hear Mat walking down the street, heels tapping on the pavement. "You need me to pick up anything?"

"Nah, I'm good, thanks."

"See you in a bit."

Ending the call, I turned and looked at the state of the living room. Empty take away boxes littered the dining table and had fallen onto the floor. Cans and bottles, some on their sides, covered the coffee table in front of the sofa. Remnants of food I hadn't bothered to throw away, stuck to the carpet. I lived in a pig sty. While I waited for Mat, I made a half-hearted attempt at clearing up. I grabbed a black bin liner from the kitchen and chucked in as much of the debris as I could.

The intercom buzzed and I shoved the rubbish bag by the front door to remind me to take it out later and went to answer it.

"Come straight up. I'll leave the door open."

A few minutes later, the door banged shut as I plumped up the cushions on the sofa, trying to make it look as normal as possible.

"Fucking hell, Scott, it smells like a cross between a brewery and a Chinese takeaway in here." Mat appeared in the doorway, a carrier bag in one hand. "I brought fresh supplies, although it doesn't look like you need them."

"Thanks, buddy." I took the bag from him and grabbed two bottles of beer from it, cracking them open with the bottle opener I just happened to have in the pocket of my jeans.

"I'm slightly nervous to sit on that couch." Mat pointed to the leather sofa with the top of his bottle. "You've been on your own way too long."

"Fuck off." I tossed a cushion at his head, then unfolded the throw over the back and opened it up over the seats. "Better?"

He laughed. "Only kidding, mate. We've experienced worse, right?"

We sat down, silence descending between us. Mat was doing the right thing, checking up on me, making sure I wasn't about to do anything stupid.

"Oh, you need to listen to this." He pulled a USB stick from his pocket. "Music for the new tracks. Wanted you to hear it before putting down the vocals. Think we've got several really strong single options that will get heaps of radio play." He grinned. "Funnily enough, we seem to get a lot more done when you aren't there."

I took the stick from him. "Cool, I'll listen to it later."

"Make sure you're sober when you do."

"Why wouldn't I be?"

"Don't think I didn't see the bag of rubbish by the door when I came in. Have you had people over?"

Avoiding his gaze, I shook my head. It would have been so much easier to get him to think that and I wasn't verging on an alcohol and weed problem. For years, I'd teetered on the brink of something more damaging, but always managed to pull myself back before I fell too hard.

"How are you, Scott?" Mat's head bowed as he asked so he could meet my gaze.

We didn't often do emotion or feelings. More often than not, it was a slap on the back or a joke or something which didn't require us to acknowledge what was really going on. For Mat to actually ask the question directly must have meant he was really worried about me. If I carried on down this self-destructive path, he would probably have every right to.

"I'm fine, really." I forced the words out, knowing every one of them was a lie.

"You're not though, are you?" Mat gestured around the room. "This isn't normal behaviour, even for you. In the past, when you've taken yourself out of the picture and gone to your Mum's house, you've come back full of inspiration and energy. Sure, we got the songs, but something's missing. What's happened?"

The realisation I love Rosie Tatton is what's happened.

"Nothing. I spent a bit of time with Rosie, my aunt and my cousin. We had fun." I lifted the beer bottle to my mouth and tipped the contents down my throat.

Mat twisted his own bottle around in his hands. "Sorry, mate. I don't believe a word of it. Something happened there. Did you fall out with your family or something?"

He was so far off the mark, it was untrue. Although I should have torn into Bas for going ahead with the shoot with Rosie. Even though she'd treated me to a sneak preview of the original shots, seeing the finished version - where Bas had his hands all over her - made me unreasonably jealous. It seemed I couldn't look at any form of social media without their faces, and Rosie's tits, being plastered all over it. Which made me want to do bad things.

I stretched out my neck and waved the USB stick at him. "Am I going to be blown away by the content on this?"

"Course you are, mate. Would you expect anything less?" Mat grinned. "But stop changing the subject. "Look, when we last talked, when you were at the studio, I suspected something was going on. You brushed me off then, but I'm not leaving until you tell me the truth."

Shit. Mat had a stubborn streak much like mine, and if he said he wasn't leaving, I'd be stuck with him until I told him something he believed. Aside from Bas, he was my best mate. We hadn't been in a band all these years for me to fob him off with something which had the potential to change the course of my life. Of our life, if I thought about it.

Draining the rest of my beer and opening another bottle, I let out a hard breath. "Truth is, there is nothing going on with me and Rosie. Which is pretty much the problem, because I think I'm in love with her."

A loud whistle filled the room. "Shit, man! I knew there was something strong between you two, but I had no idea!"

"There's one slight snag though. She has absolutely no idea." I dragged a hand through my still damp hair. "And I'm so fucking gutless, I haven't been able to tell her."

"No wonder you've been off your game." Mat shook his head. "Wait until I tell the others."

"No." My tone was firm. "I don't want anyone else knowing." I sighed. "At least not until I've plucked up the courage to tell her and found out how she feels about me. For all I know, it's a one-way crush."

"Unlikely. I've seen the way she looks at you. Not seen her since Brixton, but her eyes never left you throughout that whole gig."

Mentally, I face palmed myself. If only I'd noticed on the night, instead of ending up in some bar. I should have gone out with Rosie and Saff.

"For once in my life, I don't know what to do."

Mat slapped me on the shoulder. "You'll work it out, Scott. You always do."

This time, I wasn't so sure.

30

ROSIE

"Trust you to have a room in the hotel, even though you only live ten minutes away."

I raised an eyebrow. Saff hadn't objected too much when I said she and Tris could use it as a base for the evening. It had come as a surprise when Saff had told me Vivian had invited her to the dinner as well. I didn't know they knew each other, but she had mentioned Jonas and the record company were also involved in the charity.

"It's something you'd do, Saff. So people in glass houses..." Tris let his jibe trail off.

He looked gorgeous in his tuxedo, even if he complained every two minutes that the collar was too tight and that he couldn't breathe. Saff had chosen a black lace, gothic inspired number with a tight pencil skirt that ended just below her knees. I'd gone all out on the sparkle: a gold sequinned mini dress, with a high neckline and hit mid-thigh, but when I turned, it was backless, the drape of the fabric dipping right to the curve of my arse. From the front, fairly prim and proper, and daring and reckless from behind.

Since seeing Vivian, the previous week, we'd got into the routine of chatting almost every other day. She hadn't pressed me to confront Scott, and I hoped that subject was now closed. When I'd suggested bringing a date, she'd brushed it off with a comment about limited ticket availability. I wondered if she was trying to set me up with Bas instead.

When we got to our table, which was front and centre, it didn't surprise me to find I was seated next to him, with Tris on my other side. As I circled the table, seeing who else was sitting with us, I froze when I saw Scott's name on the place directly opposite mine.

What the hell was he doing here? And why had no-one told me?

My head spun around, trying to find Saff or Bas.

I spotted Saff chatting to a bunch of women near the stage and crept up to them. Plastering a fake smile on, I took Saff's arm. "Sorry, do you mind if I steal her away?"

Once we were a safe distance from them, Saff breathed a sigh of relief. "God, thank you for saving me. If I got asked another time who designed my dress, I might have screamed. I'm not sure Top Shop was the answer they were looking for."

Ignoring her apparent distress, I got right to the point. "What are you doing here? Why were you invited?"

"Bit harsh, Rosie. I am allowed to come to these posh events too. You don't have the monopoly on them." She sniffed.

"Sorry, I didn't mean it like that." I tucked a strand of hair which had come loose from its bun back behind my ear. "Scott's here."

Saff bit her lip. "Yeah, I know." She picked at a piece of skin next to her thumbnail. "I'm not meant to tell you."

"Tell me what?"

She pointed to the stage. "There's entertainment after dinner."

"Yeah, some comedian and a dance troupe who won one of those talent shows." I could tell she was wrestling with herself as to whether to tell me the truth. Whoever had sworn her to secrecy had done a pretty good job for once.

"Plus a couple of musical acts." She let out a hard breath. "Vivian will kill me."

"Why will I kill you?" As if on cue, Vivian materialised beside us. She looked resplendent in pale pink Chanel, which floated around her body with effortless elegance.

"I'm trying not to let the cat out of the bag about the music." Saff shifted from side to side, glancing over my shoulder.

Vivian placed a hand on my arm. "Patience, my dear. All will become clear later on."

I turned my head to see Scott, Tris and Bas cutting a path through the crowd. All three of them were dressed in tuxes, looking like an upmarket version of the '*Reservoir Dogs*' cast. My breath caught. I'd never seen Scott dressed in anything so smart. He looked hot as hell. *Damn.*

"Ladies," said Bas. "It's time for us to take our seats for dinner." He placed a hand at the base of my spine, his fingers grazing my bare skin. An involuntary shiver broke down my back, although I wasn't entirely sure I could attribute it all to his touch.

We all sat down, and I found myself staring straight into Scott's eyes. It was all I could do to tear my gaze away and engage in conversation with Tris.

"Andy said he'd tried to get hold of you a couple of times, but he keeps getting through to some chap who works in finance," he said, pouring me a glass of water.

"Really?" I shook my head, pretending not to have any idea what he was talking about. "I was surprised not to hear from him after we had such a fun night." I raised my voice to make sure it could be heard above the chatter, in particular making sure Scott could hear every word.

"Why don't you try and give him a ring instead?" Tris reached into his pocket for his phone. "I can give you his number."

"Sounds good." I forced a smile. "Remind me later. It looks like they're starting to serve dinner." Thankfully, a plate of roasted lamb, dauphinoise potatoes and red cabbage was placed in front of me, deflecting the awkwardness of the situation. I didn't want to see Andy again, and I definitely didn't want to give him any false sense of hope.

Each forkful of the delicious lamb stuck in my throat. Any appetite I'd had disappeared at the sight of Scott. Bas provided good company, regaling me with stories of his nightclub adventures and tales of reality TV star public appearances. While we spoke, I could feel Scott's gaze boring into me. A mixture of anger and regret fizzed through my bloodstream. Perhaps he needed to feel what I did. Making sure he could see what I was doing, I placed a hand on Bas's arm and threw back my head with laughter.

"What? It's not that funny." Bas regarded me with a strange look.

"Sorry, I couldn't help myself." I giggled, shuffling a little closer to him. I grabbed my empty glass. "Could you get me some more champagne? I seem to have drunk this a little too quickly."

"Sure." He motioned to one of the waiting staff, who hovered nearby holding a full bottle. "You should probably eat something too, soak up a bit of the alcohol."

Obediently, I shoved a forkful of the cabbage into my mouth, trying to pretend it didn't taste like cardboard. Hopefully the dessert would consist of something which would liven up my taste buds. While I chewed Bas stood up, and Scott followed suit. The two of them made some excuse about going to the bar and walked away from the table. I let out a defeated breath.

When they were a safe distance away, Vivian shifted into the seat Bas vacated. "Are you okay, dear? You look a little pale."

"I didn't know Scott was going to be here," I admitted. "I wasn't prepared to see him."

"I'm sorry I didn't tell you before, but if I had, I was worried you wouldn't come."

She hit the nail absolutely on the head. I would have come up with every excuse under the sun not to show up if I'd known. But seeing him somehow cemented my feelings. They grew dangerously out of control when I was close to him. If only I felt the same in the presence of Bas or Andy.

Either of them would make a better choice, a safer option.

But I didn't want better or safe.

I wanted Scott.

"You should talk to him, Rosie." Vivian patted my arm. "It's been a while since you saw each other. Things may have changed."

I doubted it very much. In the time since I'd fled the country house, Scott had plenty of opportunities to contact me, suggest meeting up, talking things through. His radio silence spoke volumes.

"Tonight probably isn't the right time." I gestured to the other tables and hundreds of people.

"It's exactly the right time. People are in a good mood because they are doing their bit for charity, they're with friends and family, food and drink is flowing freely."

"*People* might be in a good mood, but Scott looks like he's chewing a wasp." Greedily, I downed my whole glass of champagne. Despite everything, I was determined to enjoy myself as Vivian suggested.

"You wait, he'll cheer up later."

"Why? What's happening later?"

"Wait and see, my dear, wait and see." The always enigmatic Vivian touched her nose a couple of times. "I promise, it's worth waiting for."

I screwed up my face, wondering what lay in store for the rest of the evening.

31

SCOTT

I fucking hated events like these. The stupid monkey suit choked me. I couldn't wait to change out of it later. When Vivian called and asked me to perform an acoustic set, I couldn't turn her down. She'd always supported me throughout my career, not to mention my life, so I owed it to her to return the favour. Trash Gun wouldn't be everyone's cup of tea, but toning it down and doing softer songs always worked. I'm sure I'd have the middle-aged women creaming their panties and throwing money at the stage. All for a good cause, obviously.

"Did you know Rosie was coming tonight?" I demanded of Bas the moment we were out of earshot of our table. She looked absolutely fucking amazing in that gold sequinned number. It wasn't lost on me that from the front, it covered everything yet from behind exposed smooth, creamy acres of skin. I longed to run my fingers down her spine, watching the way her lips would part.

"Sworn to secrecy, buddy. Don't think I didn't want to

warn you, but I didn't want to risk the wrath of my mother. Not for anyone, not even Rosie Tatton." Bas held up his hands.

I raked a hand through my hair. "You could have given me a clue. Although the way you're flirting with her tonight makes me think I shouldn't be here."

"Er, I think you'll find it's the other way around. She was the one flirting with me."

"Didn't seem like you were doing much to discourage her," I grunted, leaning my elbows on the bar.

"Have you tried stopping Rosie in mid-flirt?" challenged Bas. "No, I didn't think so."

It felt like eons ago since I had actually been flirting with Rosie. Happier times, before everything had become so messed up between us. Before I'd caught feelings.

"I need a proper drink," I declared. "Can I have a double whisky on the rocks?" I asked the barman.

Bas shook his head. "Like that's going to help."

"If it gets me through this evening, it'll help."

Before we went back to the table with the wine, I downed a second double. The heat burned through my body, giving a pleasant buzz, calming the nervous energy. Despite the compulsion for getting obliterated, I had to honour my commitment to Vivian and get through the set. It was three songs. Even I couldn't fuck it up.

An hour later, Saff and I were in one of the conference rooms which had been set up for us as a dressing room. My electric acoustic sat waiting. At times like this, I wished Declan were here. He was much the better guitar player and the nerves were starting to kick in. The three songs we had planned included *Wasted By My Side*, which was why Saff was here. We'd spent an afternoon together earlier in the week going through it to make sure we knew what we were doing. As an acoustic number, it was slower, we wanted to ensure the cadence was right. I also planned to debut *Adjust My Reality*, the song I'd written at the house when Rosie was there. It was for her, about her, and it meant everything. It was the most nervous I'd been about debuting a new track, particularly when the person who inspired it was in the room. The last one was a cover of the Buzzcocks' *Ever Fallen in Love,* which I hoped at least some of the people in the room would have heard of. The lyrics resonated as much as ones I'd written myself. Then once those songs were done, I could escape.

"You didn't tell Rosie I was going to be here, did you?" I asked Saff, as I pulled off the suit jacket and loosened my tie.

"She wouldn't have come if I had." She bit her lip. "What's going on with you two?"

"Nothing."

"But you want there to be?"

I let out a hard breath. "You know our history, Saff. There's nothing between us any longer. We went out for a bit, we hooked up, that's it." Saying the words out loud made we want to believe it, but I couldn't.

"It's not though, is it? Something's changed." Saff studied her reflection in the mirror as she applied another layer of lipstick. "For both of you. Since you stayed at your house together."

Luckily, I was saved from having to answer by one of the

sound guys, who stuck his head through the door. "Five minutes, yeah?"

"Got it." I stripped off my shirt and trousers, standing there in only my boxers and socks.

"Jesus, Scott, do I have to see that?" protested Saff, covering her eyes.

"Oh, it's not the first time. We were on tour together, remember?"

"As if I could forget that nightmare." She rolled her eyes. "Put some clothes on."

"Sure I can't tempt you?" I gave her a twirl, shaking my arse in her direction.

A leaflet with information about Vivian's charity flew across the room, narrowly missing my head. "Fuck off."

"Honestly, with a mouth like that, I don't know what Tris sees in you."

"Funny." She gave me a sarcastic smile. "God only knows what Rosie sees in you. You must be great in bed, because it's definitely not your sparkling personality."

I wish I did know what Rosie saw in me. Without saying another word, I dressed in a pair of dark skinny jeans and a grey denim shirt with press studs, leaving a great deal of my chest on show. Like I said, it was for charity after all.

Picking up the guitar, I did a final check for tuning, and Saff and I ran through the chorus, our voices in perfect harmony with each other. I hoped it would replicate onstage.

Taking a final deep breath, I turned to her. "Ready?"

She nodded, holding out her hand for a fist bump. "Let's do this."

The two of us took to the stage, where Vivian stood at the microphone. She motioned to the crowd to quieten down and leaned towards the mic.

"Good evening, everyone." A loud cheer met her greeting. "Thank you for coming along this evening. I hope you enjoyed the dinner, with thanks to the wonderful chefs here. Now it's time to move on to the evening's entertainment. Later on, we have the amazing skills of the Tip Top Dance Troupe, as well as comedy from Brian Watts. But to start off, we have a musical interlude from my talented nephew and his friend." Vivian waved us closer. "So please welcome, Scott Lincoln from Trash Gun and Saffron Barnes from TheSB!"

Polite applause met our introduction, half the audience probably not having the faintest clue who we were. I relished the challenge of winning them over.

"Evening, everyone." I kissed Vivian's cheek and pulled the mic in my direction. "Thanks to my aunt Vivian for asking us to perform tonight. We'll keep it short and sweet, and I hope you enjoy it. This is *Wasted By My Side*." The lights dimmed as I nodded to Saff, who counted us in.

Vivian stepped off the stage and went back to the table. She sat down next to Rosie and whispered something in her ear. Rosie twisted in her seat, the light catching her dress making the sequins glitter in the semi-darkness. God, I wished I could hear whatever Vivian had said.

It took little effort to get through the song; I knew it inside out, had been playing it for years. Even singing it with Saff, who added a totally different element, it wasn't difficult.

The nerves which bubbled in my stomach were for the second number.

When the final chords ended, I strummed the guitar with a flourish. "Thanks so much to Saff for coming along tonight and singing with me." A round of more than polite applause filled the room, a testament to our performance, even if the crowd weren't necessarily familiar with the track.

"And thank you, Scott." Saff kissed my cheek. "I hope the rest of your performance is as well received." She directed a meaningful glance in Rosie's direction, then back at me.

I pretended to retune the strings of the guitar, stalling for time.

I took a deep breath, readjusting the mic in front of me.

"This is a new song, never before played in public, so I hope you don't mind indulging me. It's..." My voice trailed off. A steely resolve took over. "It's about someone who means a great deal to me. Maybe if I hadn't been a complete idiot, things would have been different. This is *Adjust My Reality*."

A silence fell over the room, almost as if the crowd were waiting with bated breath for what was to come next.

Whatever the outcome, I had to play.

32

ROSIE

The last time I'd seen Scott play, it had been at Brixton. A fully plugged in, electric, highly charged show. Seeing him onstage with just an acoustic guitar, bathed in a single spotlight made me catch my breath. I couldn't take my eyes off him.

Saff came to sit on my other side when she came off stage.

"You were fab, as always," I whispered in her ear.

She shook her head. "I'm seriously only here as the support act. It's Scott you want to watch."

Vivian placed a hand on my arm. "He really does look comfortable up there, doesn't he?" A broad smile crossed her face as she stared at her nephew with pride.

Catching the expression on Scott's chiselled features, which resembled a rabbit in the headlights, I begged to differ. While at the previous gig he'd been fully in control, owning every inch of the stage and performance, now his demeanour was softer, nervous almost.

Then he began to sing.

Quietly at first, then building up to the chorus.

As he launched into it, his gaze met mine.

Everyone else in the room melted away as I heard the words.

Not knowing if you know...
How I feel...
Is killing me...
Adjust my reality...
Make this real for me...

I swallowed hard, desperately trying to listen to the verse before he came back to the chorus again. His eyes never left mine as he sang the heartfelt words. A tear slipped down my cheek. Both Vivian and Saff took one of my hands as the song came to a crescendo, gently squeezing my fingers. Scott used his voice instead of the guitar for the big ending; he stopped playing but carried on singing. As he sang the last line, his voice cracked, and I almost broke down.

When he finished, he bent his head, breathing heavily, staring at the floor as applause broke out around the room. I wanted to rush onto the stage, take him into my arms and tell him I'd make it real for him, for *us*.

After a beat, he looked up again lifting one hand in the air to quell the noise. "Thank you. Looks like you enjoyed that one. I've got one last treat for you, if you remember the Buzzcocks."

He launched into *Ever Fallen In Love*, which couldn't have been more appropriate if he'd tried.

"Are you okay, my dear?" Vivian asked, her thumb brushing away my tears.

"I, I think so." I looked between her and Saff. "Did you both know about this?"

"May have had a little inkling he was up to something." Saff winked and held out a glass of champagne. "Here, drink this. You look like you need it."

My heartbeat began to return to normal as I took a tentative sip. "Where was your dressing room?" I asked Saff. "I want to be there when he comes off stage."

"It's one of the conference rooms. Berkeley or something." She grinned. "Now go!"

I grabbed my bag and headed out of the dining room, along the corridor to the conference suite. My eyes scanned each of the names of the rooms until I found Berkeley. Pushing open the door, an eerie silence came from inside. When I saw Scott's discarded tux, along with a guitar case, I knew I had the right place.

Now all I had to do was wait.

My heart raced. I perched on the edge of the table, crossing my legs, trying to look provocative. Too much. This time I didn't just want to end up back in a hotel room.

A good ten minutes had passed, and I was on the verge of giving up and going back to find Saff and Vivian, when I heard the door creak.

Scott entered, alone. When he caught sight of me, he stopped. "Rosie?"

"Scott."

It was as if we were strangers, meeting for the first time.

He walked over to the table and placed his guitar in the case, taking his time closing the clasps. His back was to me and his grey denim shirt was stained with sweat from the exertions of his set. I hadn't realised an acoustic performance required so much physical effort.

Knowing I couldn't see his face or his reaction to what I was about to say bolstered my confidence. "That song... does it mean what I think it means?"

His hand froze over the final fastening, shoulders rising and falling quickly. "What did you think it means?" His tone was husky, speaking directly to my emotions as well as my body.

"That you might have feelings for me. More than friends with benefits, more than hooking up. More than fucking in a hotel room." I rushed the words out, scared if I didn't, I wouldn't be able to say them. The silence which met them had me thinking I'd got it all wrong.

He wasn't singing to me, about me, for me.

It was all about someone else.

Deliberately, he turned to face me. "You got that from the song?"

Shit. I had got it wrong.

Flustered, I slid off the table. If I'd misunderstood, I couldn't bear to be in the same room as Scott, couldn't bear the humiliation. I'd slink away to my suite and order the entire contents of the room service dessert menu.

"Sorry, I shouldn't have said that." I went to push past him, but Scott grabbed my wrist.

"Rosie, don't go." He must have felt my pulse race beneath his fingertips, it thrummed so loud it was all I could hear. "Please."

His eyes bored into mine, filled with uncertainty. I'd never seen him like this, so unsure of himself. He swallowed hard. "I've never put myself out here like this before, so bear with me. I can't do this anymore."

My hand flew to my mouth. He was going to tell me he didn't want to see me any longer, that he'd met someone else and whatever we had was officially over. I didn't want to listen to him tell me he'd moved on, and I was destined to be part of his lurid past. "It's okay, you don't have to say anything, I get it."

Scott's brows knotted together. "No, Rosie, I don't think you do." He took both of my hands in his, gripping onto them tightly. "I don't want to hook up with you any longer..."

I knew it. I opened my mouth to speak, but he placed a finger on my lips.

"I've never felt this before. I want us to try a proper relationship, a real one this time."

Instantly, my chest tightened. It was as if the air had been sucked out of the room. The words in the song, making it real for him.

It really was happening.

33

SCOTT

I had never felt more nervous in my life. Performing in front of thousands of people at gigs and festivals was one thing, but spilling my guts out to the woman I loved topped it.

"What do you say?" I removed my finger from her lips, waiting for her reaction.

Rosie's blue eyes filled with tears. I hadn't wanted to make her cry.

"You wrote a song about me?" she managed.

"About you, for you... same difference." I shrugged, trying to pretend it didn't mean as much as it did.

"No-one's ever done that for me before."

I narrowed my eyes. "And how many other rock stars have you dated?"

She let out a small laugh. "None. It's only ever been you."

I closed the distance between us, taking her hands in mine. She was shaking, the movement making her dress catch the light, truly beautiful. "If it was only ever me, then...?"

Her eyes didn't leave mine. "I might not be able to write a song for you, but I can tell you that I don't want to be with anyone else. I don't want you to be with anyone else either. Seeing you with other women hurts." She dropped her head. "And I know I only see the gossip column version of what happens, and my assumptions might not be entirely accurate, but you're Scott Lincoln, rock star."

I bent my head, resting my forehead against hers. "You might not believe me. But anything you've seen in the past few weeks, nothing happened with those women. Nothing. I've only been with you, and I only want to be with you."

A sob caught in her throat.

"When I saw you with that Andy guy, my jealousy took me by surprise. Even the thought of you with someone else killed me. But I didn't know how to tell you." I paused. "There's one way I can express myself and that's through the music. When I started writing that song, all the emotions I had flooded out. That's when I knew how to tell you."

"I need you to play it to me again," she whispered.

"Now?"

Rosie nodded. "Tell me how you feel, Scott." She drew back, gently pushing me in the direction of my guitar.

Slowly, I took the acoustic out of the case, and settled down into a chair. Rosie perched on one of the tables, her long legs stretching out in front of her. I flexed my fingers, extracted the pick from my pocket and started to play. Unable to look at her directly, I focused my attention on playing, making sure I hit every note perfectly. Throughout the whole song, Rosie's gaze never left me. When I got to the final chorus, my voice cracked.

> *Not knowing if you know…*
> *How I feel…*
> *Is killing me…*
> *Adjust my reality…*
> *Make this real for me…*

Once I'd finished, silence descended over the room until Rosie spoke.

"I'll make it real for you, Scott. I love you."

I dropped the guitar to the floor and went to her, stepping into the space between her legs. I cupped her head in both my hands, holding her gaze, wanting to savour the moment for as long as possible. "I love you," I breathed.

Our lips crashed together, and I tasted the salt on her cheeks from the tears which had spilled. Tongues entwined, hands smoothing over skin, eager, hungry. I didn't want to wait, I wanted her right now.

"Let's get out of here."

She smiled against my lips. "We don't have to. I have a room here."

"Then what are we waiting for?"

Rosie grabbed my hand and pulled me out of the conference room. We waited impatiently for the lift, unable to keep our hands off each other, until it finally arrived.

Thankfully, we were the only two people in there. My hand dipped into the back of her dress, fingers tracing her spine, feeling her push against me. The shimmering gold of the material glittered and flashed off the mirrors in the lift, catching the light as we went up to Rosie's floor.

The room turned out to be a suite, which shouldn't have surprised me. Once the door shut behind us, I span Rosie around, cradling her face in my hands.

"Are you sure about this? About us?"

"Scott, you wrote me a song and sang it in front of hundreds of people. If that's not a sign of commitment, I don't know what is." Her hands grasped my wrists, nails gently digging into the flesh. "It's out in the public domain now. You can't take it back."

Commitment.

"I don't want to take it back." I dropped my gaze, so I couldn't see Rosie's reaction. "I can't explain why it's taken so long to get here. From us dating for a few weeks, then me fucking it up by sleeping with someone else—"

"To you coming to my rescue..." She tilted my head back up. "I don't see you just as a knight in shining armour. I hoped there was something more to it, and I wasn't wrong. Whatever it's taken for us to get here, being together, it's so, so right. There is nothing I could want more."

Her clear blue eyes radiated hope and optimism, something I hadn't felt in a long while.

I took her chin and dragged her towards me, meeting her full lips in a sweet, long, gentle kiss. Before, kisses had been urgent, passionate, raw; desperate to get to the next level.

This was new.

This was soft, searching, full of meaning and promise.

Rosie threaded her hands through my hair, and pulled me close, moaning into my mouth.

My hands moved to her dress, sliding it off her shoulders, exposing her breasts. She gasped against me as I took a nipple between my fingers and rolled it around, my other hand cupping her arse, tugging her towards my crotch. Her fingernails dug into my shoulders, before slipping down and yanking my shirt open. Involuntarily, I drew back. A playful smile played across her lips, making me growl with desire.

Taking a step back, Rosie shimmied out of the dress, letting it pool on the floor around her ankles, before kicking it away. She stood there, naked but for a tiny pair of lace panties. I swallowed hard. It wasn't the only thing that was hard. My cock strained against the fly of my jeans and I didn't know how much longer I could wait before being inside her.

I no longer needed to wait.

We were together now, there was no need to play games.

I dipped into the back pocket of my jeans, and located my wallet to find a condom, then struggled out of my clothes. Damn, a hot erection made it more difficult than it needed to be.

"Scott..."

One word was all the invitation I needed. I pushed her back onto the bed, spreading her legs and ripping those delicate knickers from her body. Without saying anything else, I skimmed my fingers over her clit, then along her slit, feeling how wet she was already.

"Please, I want to feel you inside me." Rosie lifted her hips, wriggling around impatiently underneath my touch.

"Patience, all good things come to those who wait."

"I don't want to wait. I want to come now." She pouted.

I held back a laugh; her neediness was adorable.

Slowly, deliberately, I slid between her lips, the friction already getting me close. I controlled the rhythm, teasing her as I withdrew right to my tip, then lunging straight back in again.

I risked a glance at her. Eyes closed, back arched to take me as deep as she could, teeth biting down on her lower lip as she clutched at the sheets, so close to her own release. *Fuck, she was sexy.*

The visual tipped me over the edge, with one final thrust, I came hard, collapsing next to her, my breath coming in short bursts.

Afterwards, we lay there, neither of us saying a word, revelling in what had happened.

"Isn't this normally about the time you leave?" Rosie buried her nose into my neck, teeth nipping at the skin there.

"Babe, I'm not going anywhere. It's you and me. Together, forever." My fingers tangled in her hair, pulling her closer. I breathed in the scent of her shampoo and perfume and let out a contented sigh.

We spent the rest of the night wrapped in each other's arms, chatting about the future and making tentative plans. Rosie fell asleep first, as dawn broke. I lay there staring at the ceiling, trying not to move and wake her.

This was a massive step for me. Never before had I committed to one woman so completely.

Anxiety prickled at my thoughts.

I meant everything I'd said to Rosie last night, every single word. Including the 'L' word.

She really was the only one I wanted, that I could see a future with.

And it scared the fuck out of me.

Carefully, so as not to disturb her, I slid from the bed, pulled on my clothes and headed out the door.

34

ROSIE

I rolled over in bed, only to encounter all the space which went with being alone. Propping myself up on my elbows, I glanced around the room. The bathroom door was open, and there was no sound of anyone in there. The only clothes strewn around the room were mine.

There was absolutely no sign of Scott.

He'd done it again.

He'd run out on me.

So much for a new start.

Overwhelming disappointment flooded through me and I slumped back on the pillows. Why had I believed him last night? Why did I think this time would be any different?

I should have known better.

Throwing the duvet back, I got out of bed and searched the room for my bag. Finally locating it under the sofa, I found my phone and switched it on. Several messages appeared on the screen.

Saff: Well? What's going on? You never came back after Scott's set? Tell me you're okay? Xxx

Bas: Saw you sneaking off with Scott. Hope you had a good night! ;o)

Vivian: Hope you and Scott sorted everything out. I'll see you both soon x

Defeated, I threw the device down on the sofa.

How could I have been so stupid to think Scott had changed?

Swayed by declarations of love and the most incredible sex of my life, my traitorous body had been the one to respond. I should have listened to my head.

I padded across the room to the bathroom and hooked the hotel robe off the back of the door, wrapping it tightly around my frame. If I packed up now, I could be back home within the hour. Then I could get on with my life. The gold sequinned dress was in a heap on the floor. Part of me wanted to leave the garment in the hotel. Seeing it again would only bring back memories of what could have been.

"Ugh!" I let out a frustrated scream. Fuelled by a desire to get the hell out of the room, I stomped about grabbing clothes, makeup and toiletries, before tossing them all into my suitcase. I'd sort out them when got home. Then I could work on the mess that was my heart.

While I was in the bathroom getting the last few bits, I heard the door to the room open. Expecting it to be housekeeping, I called out. "I'm still here, can you come back later?"

The door slammed shut and I piled up my things in my arms, before exiting the en-suite.

When I saw someone standing in the centre of the bedroom, I let out a shriek, dropping everything onto the floor.

"Do you really want me to come back later?"

Scott held up a Pret carrier bag. He looked deliciously rumpled in his suit, hair awry, stubble darkening his jaw.

The bottom dropped out of my stomach. "I thought you'd gone."

"Why would I do that?"

"Oh, I don't know. Maybe because of your track record?"

He stepped towards me, raking a hand through his hair. "Rosie, last night, and this morning too, I told you I love you. I'm not going anywhere."

"When I woke up and you weren't here, I thought…" I bit my lip. I'd made the assumption he'd run out again. "I thought this, us, was all too much for you and you'd changed your mind."

Scott let out a throaty laugh. "As if. I brought us breakfast." He opened up the bag and let me look at the contents. "I can't quite replicate our first breakfast together, because they don't sell pancakes, but I hope there's something in here you'd like."

"Fuck breakfast, there's something standing right in front of me I'd like." Taking the bag from his hand, I dropped it onto the table before wrapping my arms around his neck. "I may need to work up an appetite."

"Rosie Tatton, you're insatiable."

"I don't see you resisting though…" My lips met his, inhaling his familiar smoky taste. His arms slid around my waist, coming to rest on my hips, pulling me flush against his erection.

Both of us were desperate to taste the other, all thoughts of food were pushed to one side. Within seconds, our clothes were in a pile on the floor.

"I could get used to starting the mornings like this," I sighed, snuggling up to Scott.

Scott brushed a strand of hair away from my face. "Me too."

There was a knock on the door. "Housekeeping."

Another shriek escaped my lips and I grabbed the robe I'd discarded, not wanting anyone to see me naked.

"It's okay, I made sure I put the security latch on," Scott whispered, his lips brushing my neck.

Sure enough, the door opened only a few inches and a voice said, "Oh, I didn't realise you were still here."

"We'll be checking out soon," I called back. "Sorry for the inconvenience." I breathed a sigh of relief once it closed again.

"Hungry now?"

"For you? Always." The corner of my mouth pulled up and I leaned over and kissed the tip of Scott's nose. "And for breakfast now too. Time to wait on me." I shoved him out of bed.

Naked, he padded over to the table and I admired the view. Satisfaction settled over me.

"I didn't know what you wanted, so I pretty much got their entire breakfast menu."

He wasn't wrong, the bag bulged with croissants, sweet

and savoury, porridge, fruit and an acai and almond butter bowl. There were also two coffees, which had gone cold.

"You really did cover everything."

"Shame there's no syrup to cover you with." Scott winked, reminding me of our first breakfast together at his country house.

"Seriously, Scott, if you carry on like this, we'll never leave this hotel room!"

His expression grew serious. "I have one condition if we're going to make a go of this relationship."

My brows knotted together. "No syrup in bed?"

He laughed, shaking his head. "No more hotel rooms. Unless it's for very special occasions of course. I don't just want to shag you and leave you. I'm in this for the long term. If you want it too."

Scott's single stipulation for our relationship going forward was one I was totally prepared to accept. I threw my arms around his neck, scattering the breakfast options across the bed. "Oh, I want it. More than anything."

EPILOGUE

"I'm not living in Manchester." Rosie threw down the property particulars on the coffee table. She shifted position and sat with her legs stretched out on the sofa, her back against the arm.

"Wait, what?" My head snapped around to face her. "What's wrong with Manchester?"

She hefted a sigh. "My life's in London. My agent. Castings. Easy access to transport."

"Get a new agent. And, um, didn't you fly into Manchester Airport from Paris?"

We were at Mum and Vivian's house again. After the charity dinner, we'd holed up in Rosie's house for three days before she had to fly off for a shoot. I'd headed home for a bit, spending some time in the studio with the rest of the band. The new music sounded absolutely epic and we were chomping at the bit to get it out into the world. Our management team couldn't stop praising us. This next album could really be the one to elevate Trash Gun to the next level.

"My friends are in London." Rosie pouted. "I don't know anyone up here."

"What about Ellie from *SFU*? I'm sure she'd be happy to give you more work, given the success of the last campaign." I winced, realising it might remind her of the crap with Mark. In some ways though I had to be grateful to the bastard for getting us together.

"I can't only do lingerie work."

I swept my gaze over her body, clad in one of my old Trash Gun merch t-shirts. Cut deep at the sides, I caught a subtle glimpse of side boob and my dick twitched. "Oh, I don't know…"

Rosie threw a cushion at my head. I ducked to one side, then leapt on her, pinning her body underneath mine.

"I wouldn't mind if you did though." My lips hovered dangerously close to hers. It certainly hadn't done Jason Statham any harm being hooked up to a Victoria's Secret model.

"Seriously, you two, do you ever get dressed?" Bas' voice floated into the living room, totally ruining the mood. "Not exactly the best way to greet your guests."

Reluctantly, I lifted myself and returned to the upright position, careful to ensure no-one could see my growing erection. I grabbed the cushion Rosie had thrown at me and placed it in my lap to be sure.

"You're the only one here so far."

"Our mums are meeting at the station." Bas threw his holdall down on the floor. "And what about your other friends?"

"Saff said she'd text me when they're on the train," said

Rosie, rearranging my t-shirt to cover herself up too. "Knowing how great she is at time keeping, don't expect them any time soon."

What had seemed like a good idea at the time, to invite our closest friends and family to the house for a party, now seemed like the wrong decision. I wanted Rosie all to myself, uninterrupted alone time.

Not to mention the enormous elephant in the room in that I'd never introduced my mum to any of my girlfriends before. Never, in twenty eight years. Then again, I hadn't actually had someone I'd thought worthy of the title.

Rosie was worth everything.

"I guess we should get ready," said Rosie, lifting herself off the sofa, but not before giving me a little flash of the bright pink lacy knickers she wore. "I'll get in the shower first."

"I could join you? We'd save time?" I perked up at the thought.

"Scott, we would never save time if we showered together." She grazed the side of my head with her lips.

"Ugh. Too much information." Bas wrinkled his face up. "I'm going to get a coffee. Was at a new club opening last night and didn't get back until after four."

They left the room together, chattering about the club Bas had been to. I sank back onto the sofa, letting my head fall back and stared at the ceiling.

This whole relationship thing had me behaving like a teenager again. Sweaty palms, hitched breath, inappropriate erections. All of it could be attributed to Rosie.

Two hours later, the house felt crowded. I'd been used to

it being fairly empty, usually me and maybe one or two others. But with friends and family, it suddenly had the ambience of the party house it was meant to be.

Rosie looked absolutely gorgeous in a flower-patterned dress, which clung to every single one of her curves, and flowed down to just below her knee. She'd paired it with white Converse, keeping it casual. Her blonde hair was in a half-up, half-down do, tendrils framing her face. It had me itching to sweep them behind her ear, taking the time to trace a line down her jaw.

Being in love had turned me into a complete sap.

Love.

It still seemed strange to use the word.

One which hadn't been in my vocabulary until now. Until Rosie.

"Scott." Fingers caught my elbow.

I turned to see Mum smiling at me. We'd not had the chance to speak since she'd arrived with Vivian. On arrival, they'd promptly taken two gin and tonics into the garden, and only returned a few minutes ago.

Glassy eyes made me think the drinks had been more gin than tonic, but I was hardly one to complain.

"Vivian's been telling me about Rosie."

I glanced over to where the pair stood, heads bent close together, chattering away. Rosie hadn't shared much of her relationship with her own mother, so I had no idea whether they were close.

"She's…" I stopped. I honestly couldn't put into words what she meant to me. There were superlatives, meaningless phrases which ultimately meant nothing to anyone else.

"I know, Scott." She drew me into a hug, filling my head with her familiar perfume. "I can see simply by the way you look at her how much she means to you. I've never seen you look so happy."

Rosie caught my eye, and I waved her over. When she arrived, I pulled her close to me, snaking a hand around her waist. "Rosie, this is my mum."

"Lovely to meet you Mrs Lincoln." She beamed and leaned forward to place a kiss on each of Mum's cheeks.

"Oh, God, please don't call me that! It makes me feel old. My name's Ava." Mum laughed.

"Okay... Ava."

"It's lovely to finally be introduced to Scott's girlfriend too. You're the first one I've ever met."

I clapped a hand over my eyes. "Way to make me feel like a teenager."

Mum raised her eyebrows. "It's the truth though, isn't it?"

The things Rosie and I had done were anything but teenage. Although I wasn't about to share that little gem with Mum.

"When there are less people around, I'd love to get to know you better," Rosie said. "Vivian's told me a little about you too." She gave a shy smile and I wondered exactly how much Vivian had said.

"There you are!" Saff broke into our reunion, dragging Tris behind her. "Sorry we're late, we missed the train." She pulled Rosie away from me.

"If we lived in London, we wouldn't have to put up with

Saff's tardiness." Rosie turned to me, a smile playing on her lips.

"You're saying that's a plus?" I bit my lip, trying not to laugh.

Mum waved her empty glass around. "I'm going to find Vivian. We'll talk again later, Scott. Rosie, you and me too." She kissed both of us and then disappeared.

"She seems nice," Rosie whispered in my ear.

Looking around the room, seeing how many people were here - Mum, Vivian, Bas, Saff and Tris, Mat, Dev, Bobby and their respective partners - made me wonder why it had taken me so long to embrace everyone, why I'd always kept people at a distance.

Hell, why I'd kept Rosie at a distance.

Opening up and telling her everything I'd kept locked up in my heart for so long had been a revelation. Even if that had come through a song. Realising what a person meant to me, not having to look for meaningless hook ups or one-night stands, being with one woman, committing solely to her, scared the absolute shit out of me.

But as I looked over at Rosie, a stab of love piercing my chest, I knew I didn't need to be scared any longer.

WISH YOU ONCE MORE

Keep flipping to read the first two chapters of *Wish You Once More*, the story of Scott's bandmate, Mat and his first love, Bree, an angsty, second chance romance story. Out on 7th October 2020, you can preorder here: mybook.to/WYOM

The more you love someone, the more you hurt them...

Bree
Mat Redmond chose his career over me. *He broke my heart.*
I vowed never to let him affect me again.
Until he shows up in the last place I expect him to.
Old memories and feelings come back to haunt me and I can't push them away. When Mat abandons me a second time, I'm not sure I can forgive him again.

Mat
Bree Sheridan was my first love. *And I broke her heart.* I hurt her with my choices and vowed never to do it again.

Except I did, and I regret every single moment.

But when my family needs me, I have to come back home to look after them. If I make another wrong choice this time, I'll lose Bree forever.

Preorder here: mybook.to/WYOM

Chapter 1 - Mat

"What do you say, little bro? Are you in?"

The answer to Jonny's question should have been simple.

Sorry, no, Jonny. The timing isn't great and I'm not sure our manager would approve of me taking a week off to play a gig with my brother for a tiny festival no-one's heard of. Not to mention how pissed off Scott would be.

Harsh, but true.

But the words which came out of my mouth totally contradicted my thoughts.

"Yeah, sure. Sounds like a blast."

"Brilliant! Thanks, Mat. You don't know what this means."

I did, actually. It would mean a shitload of increased interest in the festival, which our hometown didn't always relish. Having the bassist from Trash Gun take up the vacant slot in his brother's band was as newsworthy as it got. Jonny babbled on about how much he looked forward to seeing me, how my sister-in-law and nephew would appreciate me being around for a while, not to mention Dad.

"Look, J, I've gotta go. We're on deadline here, and if we don't get these tracks down, we won't hit the release dates." While I enjoyed chatting with Jonny, now wasn't the time.

"Sure, give me a call later and we'll sort out all the details."

We said our goodbyes and I ended the call, a sinking sensation in my stomach.

Scott would kill me.

As if on cue, he appeared at the door to the studio's kitchen. We'd already had several heart-to-hearts in here, when he was sorting things out with Rosie Tatton, his now girlfriend. It seemed odd seeing Scott so settled, much calmer than the loose cannon he used to be. Maybe he wouldn't flare up as much as I feared.

"You okay, buddy?" he asked, stepping up to the counter and pouring himself another coffee. For Scott, caffeine was about as far as the addictions went these days, unless you counted the joints we sometimes wound the day down with.

"All good." I waved my phone at him. "My brother wanted to ask me something."

"How's Jonny doing? I haven't seen him in years."

If I had to guess, it would probably be around two years. In the past, we used to go down to my hometown by the river during summer breaks from uni. Manchester wasn't as pretty, plus we had the advantage that my family ran a holiday home business. We had often taken advantage of a last minute break if there was a cancellation. But since Trash Gun had rocketed up the popularity charts, visits had become a lot less frequent. I hadn't been home since Christmas, and even then I'd only been there three days, and barely left the house.

When Jonny told me his bassist was leaving his band to move to Bristol, which was shit timing for their most celebrated gig of the year, I knew what he'd be angling for. The band played the Dart Sundowner without fail every year, and had done since he was twenty and I was eighteen. Back then, neither of us had any idea how things would pan out. If I'd been a betting man, Jonny would have been the one fronting a rock band—he certainly had the talent—and I'd be the one maintaining rental properties and organising cleaning rotas. A guest appearance from one of indie rock's most popular bassists—I had the internet magazine's award to prove it—would ensure a record breaking audience in attendance. Ha, who was I kidding? I was no Dave Grohl. But it would probably increase donations and merchandise sales. I hadn't meant to say yes to Jonny. But I had. Now I had to deal with the consequences.

"Yeah, he's good." I hesitated. I needed to gauge Scott's mood before telling him. Fireworks wouldn't be pleasant.

"Is he still playing in that band? The JRs or whatever they're called."

Jonny had thought it amusing to name the band after himself, not realising that his initials were also a hugely famous soap opera character from the eighties. Mum had taken great delight in educating him on all things Dallas. I'm pretty sure he only started wearing a stetson at gigs to take the piss out of its origins.

"He is. They're doing the festival again this year."

Scott sipped from his mug. "We should go down and

support him. Be nice to take Rosie down there and show her some of my childhood."

I swallowed hard. "I've already said I'll go."

"Cool, can you arrange a house for us? Get your dad to sort us something out on the waterfront?"

The floor was suddenly riveting and I avoided Scott's gaze. "Sure, shouldn't be too much of a problem." I dragged a hand through my hair.

"What aren't you telling me, Mat?"

My head snapped up. "Nothing. It's nothing."

"You're acting shifty. What's going on with Jonny? Or is it your Dad?"

Thankfully, it wasn't to do with Dad. His health wasn't the best, and every time Jonny called I panicked, thinking something had happened. When Mum passed away, Jonny and I were young, and Dad had been there for us ever since. We were tight. The Three Musketeers, until I deserted them for university in Manchester, and started playing in a band with Scott. The rest, as they say, is history.

"Dad's fine, it's…"

Shit, why was it so hard to tell Scott?

"I'm going to play in Jonny's band at the festival," I blurted out.

There was a moment of silence. Scott took another sip of coffee and I waited for the explosion. He nodded. "You are?"

I wished there was a beer around or something to wet my dry mouth with. Instead, I grabbed a bottle of water from the fridge, and gulped it down.

"What happened to his bassist?" asked Scott. His tone

seemed calm enough, but it didn't mean he wouldn't mouth off at any moment.

"Moved to Bristol. Came out of the blue, apparently. His girlfriend got a new job there and it was too good an offer to turn down." The explanation sounded lame. After all, musicians travelled the length and breadth of the country for gigs, so what was one more in his hometown? But his girlfriend had threatened to leave him if he didn't move with her. True love won out, leaving Jonny in the lurch.

"Right. Not exactly committed to the cause then. And clearly doesn't possess my excellent persuasion skills." Scott quirked an eyebrow.

When Scott and Rosie got together, she had been adamant that a move to Manchester was definitely not on the cards. Fast forward a few months, and the couple had settled in one of the trendiest apartment blocks in the city. Rosie still kept her place in London, renting it out to some trustworthy friends, but she had definitely settled up north.

I frowned. "But you're okay with me playing the gig?"

Scott spread his hands. "Who am I to stop you?"

"I thought there might be something in our contract, which prevented me from doing it?" I omitted to mention I thought Scott might stop me too.

"You could check with Tobias if you're that worried?"

Our manager usually didn't like us bothering him with things like that. Unless it meant an imminent arrest or law suit, he wasn't interested.

"Will you be getting paid?"

I chuckled. Scott ought to know enough about the Dart Sundowner to realise that The JRs played for drinks, not money. As our family business contributed significantly to the coffers of the festival in substantial donations, it seemed crazy to expect payment. Particularly when we reaped a lot of benefit from the people who stayed in the town over the weekend in our properties.

"Only if Jonny slips me a few quid."

"Then it shouldn't be an issue." He shrugged. "Like I said, I'm not gonna stop you. But you do have to arrange a shit hot house for us."

I liked this new, less angry version of Scott. Rosie had done a lot to smooth off some of those spiky edges. He seemed a lot more chilled, a lot less angry.

"You got it."

"Now, are we going back in there to get this EP done?" Scott threw the remains of his coffee into the sink and dumped his mug into the dishwasher. Seriously, he'd changed.

"Yeah, gimme a sec, I'm going to get a drink." I faffed about with a mug, spooning coffee into it, and stalling for time.

When I was alone, I contemplated exactly what I'd let myself in for agreeing to play at the festival. While spending time with my family and catching up with some old friends for a few days would be great, there would be ghosts of the past I'd have to deal with. Ghosts I'd successfully managed to avoid the last few times I'd been home.

One in particular.

Going home for the festival would mean seeing Bree Sheridan again.

Chapter 2 - Bree

"You'll never believe what I've just heard." Darla Charlton dumped her bag on the table with a flourish before sitting down.

"If it's juicy gossip, can we wait until everyone's here?" I gestured around the table at the vacant chairs. "That means you only have to say it once."

Darla huffed, and rummaged around in her bag for her notebook and pen. "Okay," she grumbled. "Where is everyone anyway?"

Tonight was the last committee meeting before the Sundowner. It would be the last chance for us to make sure everything was in place, that there were no last minute drop outs, and that everyone knew exactly what they were supposed to be doing across the course of the two days. For a small team, we were a well-oiled machine, and we all knew our places.

This year, I was tasked with looking after the main information point, where we also sold various pieces of merchandise. One of the more important roles, I was grateful to Darla for giving me the opportunity. In previous years, I'd been assigned the more menial stuff, like clearing up the area around the stage or collecting cups. She always said it was good to get the 'youngsters of the town' involved. At twenty-six, I wasn't sure I still qualified to be in that group, but I'd take it.

Five minutes later, the eight members which made up the committee had settled down at the large table in the private dining room of The Castle Hotel. Darla, as chair, cleared her throat to start the meeting. "So, I mentioned there was some big news," she began.

"It sounded more like gossip to me," mumbled Bryan, who took on the technical side of things, and believed in factual stuff, not gossip or tittle tattle.

"Whatever." Darla held up a hand. "You know how The JRs always play in the Sunday afternoon slot?"

My heart jumped into my mouth. Jonny Redmond's band always gave me the feels, and not always for the best reasons. Had something happened to them? They were a popular, timeless part of the festival, if they weren't playing, then...I didn't want to think about it.

"Their bassist has left."

A collective gasp went around the room. If that was true, then we suddenly had a vacant slot in the programming, which wouldn't be an easy one to fill. Everyone started talking at once, asking what the alternatives were, how we were going to explain the gap, how difficult it would be to get a replacement at this late stage. I didn't get involved, choosing instead to wind a strand of silver-blonde hair around my finger.

Darla slammed her palm on the table, causing us to jump. The volume immediately went down. "But we have no reason to worry, because they have a stand in, who has agreed to play so we aren't left in the lurch."

Murmurs bubbled up as speculation mounted as to who it was.

If it wasn't someone who was a big deal, Darla wouldn't have been making such a fuss.

If it was someone from one of the other local bands step-ping in, there wouldn't have been a need to mention it.

Which meant there was only one person it could be.

And I wasn't sure I was prepared to see him again.

"His brother, Mat, has agreed to come down for the weekend and support the festival. He'll be playing with Jonny and the others." Darla's triumphant tone grated on my last nerve.

Even though I had been pretty sure what was coming, hearing the words made my blood run cold.

Mat Redmond.

Bassist of Trash Gun.

Adored by many, but I wasn't one of them.

Not when he'd taken my heart, trampled all over it, and then thrown it away.

I reached for my glass of wine, and took a huge slug, all the noise in the room fighting for attention in my head. I couldn't let my emotions show, not now. Not when there were seven other people in the room who would question why I reacted the way I had.

"Isn't that great news?" Bryan nudged me in the ribs. "To have such a star in our midst, even if only for the weekend."

I practically spat my wine out. Other people may have seen Mat as a star, but I couldn't. Never again.

The rest of the meeting passed by in a blur. I took copious notes, trying to focus on anything that wasn't Mat Redmond, but it was almost impossible. I couldn't wait for the meeting to finish, so I could meet Callie and tell her what was going on. Surreptitiously, I slipped my phone from my pocket and messaged her to say she should have a bottle of wine waiting. She replied almost immediately, with a picture of aforementioned wine and two large glasses.

"Right, if you need anything before the weekend, please do let me know. Otherwise, I'll see you all at midday on Saturday." Darla finally brought the meeting to a close. I shut my notebook with a snap.

"Got a handle on everything you need to do?" Bryan nodded to my notebook. "There'll be lots of people wanting information."

I plastered a saccharine sweet smile on my face. It wasn't the first time he'd patronised me. "I'm sure I'll manage, Bryan. And if not, I can always ask you, can't I?"

He mumbled something under his breath, while I shoved everything into my bag.

Darla caught hold of my arm as I went to leave. "You're friends with Mat Redmond, aren't you?"

Friends. Yeah, that was it. We were friends. I bit my lip against what I really wanted to say. Taking my feelings out on Darla wouldn't help, I knew that.

Not capable of speaking, I nodded.

"Good. Can you get in touch with him and let him know how grateful we are for him stepping in at the last minute?"

Mutely, I nodded again, mentally cursing myself. Why had I agreed to that? I hadn't been in touch with Mat for ages. We hadn't exactly parted on the best of terms.

She beamed. "Thanks, love. We wouldn't want him to think we weren't welcoming. I'll see you on Saturday."

I stopped myself from nodding again and managed to forced out some words instead. "Sure. No problem."

Five days. Five days before I had to see my ex again.

No wonder I needed a drink.

Callie sat at a table in the corner of the Black Cap pub, our regular haunt. Her head bent over her phone, engrossed in whatever gossip story she'd found. Her dark hair spilled over her shoulders, which she brushed out of the way as she picked up her glass. I must have wandered into her eye line when her head jerked up and she waved.

"Where the fuck have you been? I'm starving!"

"You know where I've been, and I'm not late." I glanced at the clock behind the bar and saw it was seven thirty; I was spot on time.

"You know how grumpy I get when I'm hungry."

"You might lose your appetite when you hear what I've got to tell you." I dropped into the seat opposite her and poured myself a huge glass of wine, rewarding myself with a healthy sip. Having finished the one at the meeting, drinking more on an empty stomach wasn't the best of ideas, but I didn't care. After what I'd found out, I needed all the alcohol in the world to erase the memories of Mat Redmond.

Callie wrinkled her nose. "What's going on? Have you got a date?"

If only it were that simple. Me, having a date would be newsworthy enough on its own, but throw a certain ex into the mix and it could go viral.

"Can we order food first though? My stomach needs to know it's being fed at some point this evening." Despite us knowing the menu backwards, Callie pushed one towards me.

Diversionary tactics, brilliant. I tapped my fingers on the

table. The sooner I could tell her, the sooner she could help me formulate a plan as to how to avoid Mat for the whole weekend. It was utterly ridiculous to think I needed to avoid someone who had broken me so completely four years ago.

We ordered burgers each and decided to share a large fries, because the Black Cap's portion sizes were legendary. I wavered between the need to purge everything in my stomach and fill it with crap food.

"So, what's up?" Callie looked expectantly at me.

There was no point in sugar coating it or beating around the bush.

"Mat's coming back this weekend."

Her hand froze in mid-air, glass midway between the table and her lips, her eyes wide. "Mat Redmond?"

"How many other Mats do we know?"

She blinked. If she made me say his name one more time, I would kill her. Even thinking about him was enough to send me into a full spiral. "Why?"

"Something to do with his brother's band needing a bassist for the festival."

"Oh, yeah, I'd heard something along those lines."

That was the problem with our small town. Everyone knew everyone's business. I hated people outside of my friendship group knowing what was going on in my life, particularly when it involved an up and coming rock star.

"Why didn't you tell me?"

"I didn't know it would lead to Mat coming back." Callie wrinkled her nose. "How long's he going to be here for?"

"Honestly, I have no idea. Plus, I don't care." I crossed my fingers underneath the table so Callie couldn't see me. "If he's only coming back for the festival, it can't be more than a couple of days. So tell me, how am I going to avoid him?"

"*Honestly, I have no idea.*" Callie mimicked my response. "You're going to have to get used to the fact that you're going to see him again."

Damn. I hated it when she was right.

Preorder here: mybook.to/WYOM

ACKNOWLEDGMENTS

These are crazy times, and when I started writing Wish You Knew at the start of lockdown, I had no idea this story would give me the escapism I needed. Scott and Rosie's story was an absolute pleasure to write, and I hope you enjoy them as much as I did!

Writing is only part of the story and bringing a book to life needs an entire village.

Anna, you are much more than an editor and I'm glad I have you in my life. You've given me confidence and belief in myself and somehow 'thank you' doesn't seem enough. And yes, you may have Scott all to yourself...

Nicole, our calls may be more about life than books and coaching these days, but I couldn't do this without you. You motivate and inspire me more than you could know.

To my author besties, Jeannie, Joslyn and Roberta. Thank you for letting me rant and bounce ideas around. You're always there, and know that I'm there for you too, however hard things get.

Mr A, you are the rock to my chick. Always.

And to you, the reader, for taking a chance and reading my stories. I can't thank you enough.

ABOUT THE AUTHOR

Julie Archer is the author of contemporary romance featuring rock stars, small towns, a healthy dose of angst, some steamy times and always a happy ever after!

When not writing, I can usually be found binge watching teen drama series on Netflix, or supporting Spurs from my armchair, and running around after my two feline children, Corey and Elsa.

www.juliearcherwrites.com

You can also sign up to my newsletter or catch up with me on social media.

ALSO BY JULIE ARCHER

You can read all of my books for **FREE** on Kindle Unlimited.

The Blood Stone Riot Series

Cocktails, Rock Tales & Betrayals (The Blood Stone Riot Series Book 1) - relaunching soon!

One Last Shot (The Blood Stone Riot Series Book 2) - relaunching soon!

Wild Tonic (The Blood Stone Riot Series Book 3) - relaunching soon!

Cosmopolitan Rock (A Blood Stone Riot Short Story)

Reckless Intentions (A Blood Stone Riot Novella)

The Blood Stone Riot Series Box Set - relaunching soon!

The Love Sparkles Series

Design For Love (Love Sparkles Book 1)

Fit For Love (Love Sparkles Book 2)

The Trouble Series

Trouble

More Trouble

Big Trouble

The Trouble Series Box Set - Books 1-3

Standalones

Rivers of Ink

The Six-Week Single Dad

Where There's A Will

Love Like Crazy

Printed in Great Britain
by Amazon